OVERLOOK

A Rock & Roll Fable

PAUL SMART

RECITAL

Cover design by Bryan Maloney
Author photo © Paul Smart

Print ISBN: 978-1-7337464-9-6

Library of Congress Control Number: 2023941557

RECITAL PUBLISHING
Woodstock, NY
www.recitalpublishing.com

Recital Publishing is an imprint of the online podcast The Strange Recital.
Fiction that questions the nature of reality
www.thestrangerecital.com

"And I will sing of that second realm, where the human spirit is purged and becomes worthy to ascend to Heaven."

Dante, *Purgatorio*, Canto I

1

The mirror's clouded. I circle my palm against it; catch a glimpse of my face. Eyes pink at the corners, like they're decomposing. A shot of jaundice stretching to the iris. Blood veins spread out from two spots I scratched into the retina running through pines.

On the second swipe, I get to the meat of me. My center—nose, eyes, mouth—impossible to catch while driving. Ears and graying hair, the distinct bristle of an aged's beard beneath my beak. The edges where this motel bathroom's reflected. Fake tile; seashell wallpaper.

Late March. 1986.

I count the empty bottles of Grand Marnier on the vanity behind me. Oh, father, forgive me, could it be I downed another before retiring?

I don't much like looking in mirrors; now in my forties, I actively avoid them. Same with snapshots, photo shoots. Who needs to see skin stretched across the brainpan, cross-hatched around scared, ever-watchful eyes like some Peruvian desert seen from outer space? A bad cartoon.

Age? An alien landing strip if you ask me. Give me blackouts. The mindless smile of a deadened head when just high enough.

I step into the curtained half-light of our hotel room. Bright, Floridian Winter Park sun pierces the crack in the blinds, the part in the curtains. Highlights the disarray, the mournful rumple of bed sheets. My girl Dawn, gone. I remember she tossed her hair with a quick flick of that long, supple neck. And yes, I further recall her cold accusing eyes as I drifted back into oblivion.

The fog dissipates. She must be off for coffee. The sweet, muddy, chocolaty Joe with chicory I like down here. Later for the jolt of espressos, supplied as part of our contract by the Cheek to Cheek. Part of my bandmates' unspoken agreement to tamp down my sweet tooth, that unquenchable thirst; that need to lose it all, again and again, in a fuzzed-over land where you're nothing but a fan, the fucked-up marionette of some wicked puppeteer.

Why the fuck had we even taken this gig?

My neck's throbbing. Had last night involved more than the usual debauchery? It's not been easy these past weeks. Things have hit me hard, hung my ass out to dry.

Everyone's damned lucky I'm on this tour. I'd as soon be in bed back home in the hills, even if that meant listening to everybody telling me how good I had been, or could be, if and when I straightened out. Then and now? Reunion of what? It's a tradeoff... get me out on the road, boys, and you get my road self alongside what's left of the voice, my old record album grin. Take the buzz off, break the blackouts, and you get me sleeping, only half there. Just the shell, man, without the juice (ha ha).

I stumble towards pants, silk shirt. Not quite fitting right. Too skinny? Too bloated? Something's slipped.

Our old manager, Albert, died a few weeks ago. He'd been gone from our lives but still there, the way family sticks. In our money matters, our memories. The way we imagined futures for ourselves beyond Robbie.

I missed my dad. Told myself lies. Same with Ma.

Albert had always reminded me that the future was mine if I wanted it. Just like family and old friends would say, after my success.

Nothing free in life except death. And even *that* cost.

Grossman's heart leaped out and choked him mid-flight to London. Left the Concorde in a coffin. At his service, they had me sing Dylan's song about a prisoner's dream of release.

I think of my boy, Junior. Eleven and innocent. Still fucked up, last I spoke to him a few days back, by the NFL strike early in the past season. The sad sight of that strange plume of smoke twisting itself into hangman's knots as it dawned on him and his classmates that the shuttle take-off had gone south. Things can go wicked wrong in a flash. Challenger, indeed.

I look back to the rumpled bed. Does it spell love? Or just another emptiness that will never be filled except by the vague memory of lives lived before such emptiness. Can this be inspiration?

I should start writing shit down and not just let it bounce around in my head. I giggle at my feeble attempts at jokes, like flapping my arms to prove I can fly. To show myself I'm alive. To prove I still have songs in me, see, that thing everyone used to whisper I'd lost by playing too close to the bone.

I thump my sunken chest and do a half jig over the pile of clothes I have yet to put on.

Love of my life, bed. The stage for carnal knowledge and amorous escapading I started bragging about as soon as my pubes sprouted.

I'm slipping beyond myself. You have to write the single song, from one idea, one melody, before racing off on the concept for an entire album. Or the ways you'll spend royalties from your work of genius. You have to just start singing, on your own, as if you still mean it. You take any song, make it your own.

The bed sheets look like a furrowed, glacial landscape, Ontario without the lakes. Pillows and coverlet tossed up against the wall like some dead animal. An endless sad plain without any human form beneath the linens. Sad as me.

I want to lie down and sleep some more. Get past this fog clouding everything.

Last night, I was sure I saw my boy Junior out in the audience, seated at a shadowy table near the kitchen swing door. He seemed to have his head in his hands and instead of his mother with him, sweet Liz, he was seated next to the spitting image of my Ma, Gladys, back as she was in her thirties, around the time I first hit the road and moved out of her life once and for all.

Garth and I talked about this long after the show, then I went into it more with Levon. Was it true, I asked, that I tried speaking to her from the stage? Mumbled something from behind my keyboard?

Both told me I tried chatting up some girl half my age while her boyfriend stared me down. But yeah, they knew what that was like, seeing specters from the stage. Road jitters.

My Pa glowered from the dark the night before at some racetrack. He watched me in the unblinking way he did that time I joined the choir drunk and dry heaving, trying to stay with the hymns. Or the time he found me laughing on the floor of our kitchen, pancake batter everywhere and a grease fire burning on the stove. I know the voice in those eyes. How this attempt at revival was a trap. I should have gone to Chrysler, as he had. Married a local girl. Been more like my brothers.

I want to stay sitting but feel something pulling at me. I've got an incredible hunger deep inside. A craving that needs filling. I want coffee, a cigarette. My woman; any woman. The road.

I stand, reach over, and pop the television on. Sesame Street...God bless them all. I remember something about someone I knew guesting. Paul Simon? John Sebastian? Leonard Cohen, maybe? All I see is Big Bird with a bunch of kids on a city street. No sound. Just the hum of the air conditioner, muffling the world outside this motel, pushing me back inside my head.

I've been a horrible father. I have to get to a phone and call Junior.

Too bad there are no commercials. There's something ultra-real about those cloying ad voices, men waving their hands emphatically on either side of their faces as they implore people on the other side of the abyss, out here on the other side of the glass. Listen and buy! Feed the beast! All the same in the end, like every fucking song I ever wrote or sung. It's all a shill.

Everyone just wants to be loved a bit more than everybody else. See me and not my brothers, my sisters, my bandmates. Love me and not my kid. Feel my sadness.

Imagine a world where you could look at others' pleas for attention in your hand, endlessly. And compete with that, endlessly, too.

Big Bird races through numbers, forward to ten and back down to zero. I turn away as the alphabet starts. The large, beveled motel room mirror over the bureau has misted over, just like in the bathroom. What is this?

I want to go home to Woodstock. I want to see my boy. He still loves Muppets. Maybe he'd still laugh if I did my Cookie Monster.

I drove with him, three years old, strapped into the bucket seat beside me, back and forth across West L.A. looking to score from Mickey Twist. Liz thought we were off to a play date. I made up stories all afternoon for both our benefits, frantic for a fix.

"Imagine if every time you talked, your voice came out like Goofy's," I said. Junior howled as I reached back into a cooler filled with imported beer. "What if everything on your face turned rubbery and you looked in the mirror and saw Goofy, too? Just imagine..."

"Yeah, like your head would turn around and everything," I remember him saying through his laughter. But was he really talking by then? Is the fog encroaching?

Memory a jumble, but better than everything jamming my throat. Albert gone, planes falling out of the sky, the Challenger down, AIDS, prenups, Cinderella finally fucked.

"We will never forget them, nor the last time we saw them, this morning, as they prepared for their journey and waved goodbye and slipped the surly bonds of Earth to touch the face of God," was what the President had said. His words stuck like a Ray Charles song in my gut.

Not everything's a song. Or at least one I would feel right singing.

Knocks at the door. I'm standing in the middle of a misty room, naked as a scarecrow. I reach for a towel, wrap myself, and step forward. I open my darkness to the light.

I make out an old, badly shaven imp-dude in a moth-eaten, forest green sweater with a "Stand Back" baseball cap on his head, all five feet of him standing in the glare. He's talking something fast at me, about trouble and mountains, Woodstock, and my old ladies and even my kid Junior.

"Man, give me a moment," I tell him. "I feel like death warmed over."

The old man quiets down in the doorway as I step back into the room to the bureau and rummage around. Keys, wallet, change, slips of paper, and a pack of matches from the Gateway. Slipping on the pair of shades my hand finally finds, I turn back to the door and ask the dude to repeat what he'd been telling me. Slower this time, please.

"Your kid. I've been told to tell you he needs you. Now. He's hurting but bad, up north there where he's been living with his mom the way you left them. There was some call this morning. Something's happened, my friend. You're needed for who you been, for who you still could be. Woodstock, man. She's calling you."

He paused and caught his breath.

"THAT Woodstock, it's the real place?"

The man's mouth didn't seem to move as he talked, even though his words came clear and fast. He seemed to have shrunk within his clothes. Old, stained Chinos, three sizes too big. His gray eyes, one cataract-clouded, stared me down. But with this weird smile in them, like he knows something I don't.

"Wait, wait," I reply. "What you saying, man? You seen my lady, Dawn? I was just in the shower. She just went for coffee. And what's all this about Junior and Liz? Did I miss something?"

"What are YOU doing down here is what I should ask," says the little man. "Your lady friend, she drove out in a red rental car a half hour ago, back before lunch. It's time to up and climb the mountain, she said. But your mission's bigger than that, sir. And your time, by the look of things, has been wasted already."

What can I say? Still foggy as the mirrors inside my lonely room, still climbing out of the previous night's blackout, I'm having trouble getting a handle on the strange little dude's words.

"What you mean?" I ask the guy. "She was just going for coffee. For fuck's sake, Sesame Street's on. Junior's in fucking middle school already."

"That may be, sir, but it's after four in the afternoon. You know I been to Woodstock myself once? I was six at the time, staying at my grandma's up on the Mountaintop. She'd brought me down from Schoharie 'cause Uncle Ray was losing his best Jersey cows and didn't want me to see what needed doing. Grandma walked us down that mountain to Woodstock and back. I was scared the whole way 'bout snakes and hobos, partly because grandma had the very same fears and liked to talk them up, but good. We had hobos back then, you know."

"Wait one second," I jump in, shivering now despite the heat. "What's your name? Who are you?"

"You don't know me," the old man replies. "Call me Cato. You know I'm not what I used to be. I'm past 90 now..."

"Don't look a day over 70," I reply, deadpan.

"All I know is that your lady friend, she's gone, and I've got this other message to relay to you saying you better be headed north. And some big guy who said he was your manager said you could do what you wanted for all he cared. It was all a tragedy to him...whatever that means."

"Must be Joe," I mutter. "Joe's always talking shit like that."

"Well, sir. I better be going now," Cato adds, eyes smiling while his lips stay still. "You take care climbing that mountain now. And you treat your boy right so's his life ain't messed up like any of the rest of us now. Like I learned when I was a kid, there aren't really no snakes up there. Only on the road, while you're up and climbing. I remember it all from when I was six."

"Right," I say as he turned to shuffle away across the asphalt, the glare of Florida spring light enveloping him as he went. "I been looking to trebuchet myself out of here anyway. I miss the seasons, the slow thaw and first buds."

The man stopped, caught in the glare like a light within light.

"It's the hobos you should be scared of, son," he says. "And I believe they call it Old Overlook, I do."

I shut the door, trying to regain my bearings. The shower fog's denser. On the television, Bert and Ernie argue over the letter X. And then F, as in Friendship. Freak. Fire in the belly. Failure.

F as in Finality.

I wish they'd all just quit and go away. I'm worried about Junior. I'm worried about Liz. Dawn.

I used to pride myself on being able to read glimpses of what was going to happen down the road a few days. My Ma called it both a blessing and a curse. Like when I started sliding before the band broke up. What could I say, that I knew what was coming? Recognized the greed?

Everything feels clouded. Something's slipped inside, leaving my soul as battered-feeling as some piano that's been re-tuned with a hammer.

I have some traveling to do. Seems I must climb that mountain again, Old Overlook, and taste the sun in my hair once more.

Dredge up the old songs one last time. Figure out what the old guy meant. Save my son. Direct what's left of my life.

Oh, if only the sunlight could truly wake me now.

2

She was framed by the window. Through the trees, past the barn, over on the other side of the road catty-corner to Sid's Ford, where the strange country soul known as Klokko was parked.

She moved across the room, flowered nightie sailing before faded flower wallpaper. Klokko knew she would return, eventually. He waited, cat-like.

The wind picked up, scurrying haphazardly across the highway what leaves hadn't turned to winter mulch. Bare trees swayed under a lemon moon which glinted in the melted ice at the edge of the road and its cratered dirt pull-off. Patches of snow, gravel-encrusted and rusty-looking like an old lady's hair.

There was a scraping sound, and then something akin to breath blowing slowly over a wide-lipped bottle. A car turned off Maben Road onto the highway, splaying its beams across the house Klokko watched. Asbestos shingling in need of a paint job. Worn trim single-coated a dark green. A sloping porch with couches, dead plants, kids' toys. Big Wheels and plastic guns and roll carts.

Old, patchy leaf-mottle piled up against wind-snapped and rotting porch rails.

His pursed lips whistled: breathing out, breathing in. Klokko's free hand, lying to his right on the blanket-covered front seat of his mushy, pea-green interior '71 Oldsmobile, kept up a steady rhythm. Thumb to first finger, on to second, back to first, on to third, back to first, on to pinky. He kept it up.

The car was cold and silent except for the breathy whistles that accompanied Klokko's watching. They dispersed like a driver's thoughts in traffic as the man, bony in crumpled clothes, hawk-nosed, stubble-faced, and thin-haired, kept watch on his lady in the distant window.

Why the concept of time, he was thinking. Always waiting. Why the ageless dreams appearing, ghost-like, at key moments of one's life, drawing actions and yearnings and even the slightest thoughts into their wake like science fiction magnets, like mesmerists? We cocoon ourselves against such power in sad capsules of clothing and what passes for corpulence. In half-remembered songs and dashed dreams, like drowned-out rocker's lyrics. Melancholic feelings of failure, regrets, senses of inadequacy, and accompanying memories countered by the doubting belief that this resulting tangle somehow defined a person.

Inside the man's middle-aged head, a 14-year-old boy trapped inside a 43-year-old's body, Klokko pondered the always-present realization that his very thinking could somehow escape him, cross a cracked asphalt county road, leap over that toy-laden old porch that was hers, and sluice silently through the young girl's window and into her mind and well-hidden heart.

When he saw her, the girl he watched, and wanted her as something flesh and blood instead of the constantly inhabited heart and soul of the oh-so-many songs that lived deep in his mind, it was like his own words were handed over to his strange humming. She was rock and roll made real. A PERSON created in the supreme being's eye who was way beyond *his* images of the many hers that inhabited the tunes that lived within him, always: Gary Puckett's *Young Girl. Martha, My Dear. Close To You. Sugar Magnolia. Lady Jane.* Even Springsteen's *Fade Away*, the Police's *Every Breath You Take. Lonesome Suzie*, the first song, the ultimate she, that he'd taken in as his own simultaneous to his sprouting puberty years. Van Morrison. Klokko figured that all his songs walked in her. The tunes, their words, were a bridge, a ribbon of pure love, spanning this forgotten road between his Olds and her bedroom. Her bed. Their two hearts beating as one.

A moving frame of yellowed hall light opened onto the upstairs room's far wall. Klokko's aging, blood-streaked eyes widened slightly. His hum-whistle stopped. A halo-haired shadow appeared, turned on a table lamp.

She had thick, reddish-blonde hair loosely riding her shoulders. Soft, like a morning rain; if only his hands could but touch her, run fingers through those tresses. Just once would be enough to make the motion eternal, like a song remembered forever. The lady wore a purple nightgown with yellow flowers and mauve lace frills above her hands, which were delicate and mottled with pink. Or at least he imagined such. An adorable fragility. Barefoot and moving in quick darts and slow slides, arranging pillows on a corner bed covered in a white-tufted spread, a homemade brown and yellow afghan, several well-loved teddy bears, and assorted magazines. This is what "home" was all about, he assured himself with a quiet nod of the head.

When she moved out of view, Klokko's eyes relaxed for a moment and he breathed out, breathed in. He re-entered the fragmented world of half-remembered, fully lived-in pop songs he had inhabited for as long as he could remember. His world of half-seen newspaper headlines and half-heard news broadcasts, of overheard conversations and imagined motivations, conspiracies, insurmountable challenges...all filtered through a pop haze. Exploding rocket ships played out to a Ziggy Stardust anthem; half-clad women running from machine gun-wielding gorillas in dark, scary jungles, the sound of *Desolation Row* lamenting their every move. Arabs blowing up airplanes, and airports, as the Kinks sing *Lola*. Those Bears from Chicago and the Dead's *Bertha*, recorded out in Berkeley. The upcoming Rock and Roll Hall of Fame ceremonies, half-getting the pantheon right (set to the smiling melody of an Alka Seltzer jingle).

Klokko thought of himself within that widely warped world as a bad son, a shy would-be lover. But a knight errant still, full of chivalrous manners and gallant yearning. Rock royalty. The supreme fan driving his father's old Olds, fine-tuned as his steed.

His lady reappeared, holding a thin, slightly struggling Siamese cat. She pulled back the bed covers and sat on crisp white sheets, lips moving silently in conversation with the now settled cat in her Afghan-topped lap.

The only sound Klokko heard was that breath-like wind above, the scampering wet leaves outside, and the imagined songs of the old house across the road and its upstairs room where he could see her moving. It added up to the snanana and reedeedee of scratched LP surfaces. "Martian Applause," as he called it. The soundtrack filling his head.

It had always been so, he thought. In his attempt to become a desirable lover he had silenced himself so nothing bad could escape his defenses. Drawn deeply within, Klokko had learned to observe life silently, never touching it. And hence, never really touched by it, either.

The cat moved, stepping gingerly out of the young woman's lap. It yawned, walked over to an arms-akimbo bear, stopped. Then circled into a blanket/bear nest. She watched, lips moving in speech. She pulled her legs, momentarily bared, into bed with her. The girl fluffed pillows, shifted about, and leaned out of Klokko's frame of vision. Returned with her thumb in a hard-cover book, which she placed between her two hands on the bedspread before her chest. Her gaze sailed into the blackness of the window before her and marched directly across the night and empty snow-and-ice-edged roadway and through the Delta 88's thick wide windshield into Klokko's own. A blank thoughtful stare rested itself up against the black night's sweet reflection.

Klokko constricted with a primitive, worm-like motion. He could feel his eyes, the skin around them, his ear and inner ear, the stubbly hairs around his mouth, his drying lips, his own saliva on his own tongue, his throat waiting swallow. He could feel the rip in the fabric of his car's front seat, feel it through his dead mother's favorite blanket, which she deemed his from when he was a baby, and through his thick, quilted jeans and thin cotton underpants, as though it were newly branded into his skin. Elbows and knees and fingers and toes and every single bone in his body felt Klokko, along with the crusted, final layers of snow smothering the earth. The way his own shyness and overwhelming wish to be chivalrous—like the heroes of old he'd been dreaming of ever since his mom had read to him and his lost older brother Gerard—smothered his own better self. The way he'd smothered his own loves for thirty plus years to this point where the only woman he felt he could now love was the same age he had been when first he smothered himself so many bitter years earlier.

Sitting in his Olds, the young woman he adored staring blankly into the night in his direction, Klokko felt the peeling paint on her old house's porch, the sharp jagged edge of the broken pane of glass in the storm window before her window. And most of all, he felt the wind, whistling above the entire scene and bouncing sullenly off her house and her room, touching lightly, energy lost, against her very eyes as nothing but air.

Klokko felt his heart climb out of his body and car and into a dream-like pulpit above everything, in the sky over the roadway and almost on the same level as the young woman's window. He was able to watch his own breathing stop, his neck extending turtle-like, and his thinning-haired, elegantly nosed, stubble-faced and wide-eyed head twist clockwise in a full circle and back, counter-clockwise, to its starting position. Slow-like.

Another car's lights crossed Klokko in the parked Olds. Her light was off. Sound returned as Klokko breathed in and breathed out. The tuneless songs gelled back into a melody in his head, into a slow rendition of the old Ray Charles classic, *You Don't Know Me.*

"Never knew about making love. My heart aches," he whisper-sang, gravel-voiced and hoarse from lack of practice at the art of talking. Then back to the hum-whistling, static-like. Snanana; reedeedee. All inside his head, where his whole life existed and had been lived for decades.

Klokko started the car and let it idle a minute while looking again at his girl's beloved window, now black above the silent house. Only a flicker of blue television light escaped across the still toy-strewn porch from the living room downstairs.

He turned on the Oldsmobile's ancient 8-track. The old machinery whirred a moment before clicking into song.

"She looks my way," he whispered, dry-throated, in anticipation of where he'd left off when he shut the motor down an hour or so earlier. "She starts to cry..."

The song on the car's stereo system followed his hoarse lead, as if part of his inner life.

There are times one's life's a movie, Klokko thought. You just can't change the plot. You watch it and it takes you somewhere. Like the music that had pulled him here, to her. And eventually, he sighed, her to him. *If* the music was true.

Klokko turned on his headlights and peeled out of the potholed lot at Sid's Ford. The tires squealed on ice for a moment, then caught on the long asphalt ribboning out across the county, the state, the nation, all hooked in together like blood vessels, like life itself.

He was sick of himself and ready for change. Deep inside, something started shifting.

3

D riving blows the worries out my head quicker than any shotgun. Problems with my kid, ex-wife, and girlfriend? A reunion tour with my old band gone sour after only a month, my voice withering away as I slip off the wagon to cope with diminished crowds and sadly booked clubs in suburbs up and down the east coast? My grieving mother and angry brothers all wishing I'd been a better son?

Hit the road and I'm alright, Ma.

Instead of heading east over to I-95, I take the inland route north. Old U.S. 301 rolling up through the gentle undulations that pass for hills outside of Ocala, then deep into Florida and Georgia flatlands up through Statesboro until it hooks in with 95 at South of the Border.

Woodstock-bound, I keep telling myself. Great title for a return-to-form song. Maybe a hit if people can still remember the town I'm headed for.

Driving mind: front lobes trying not to crash and burn, back of head free to roam. A black Buick matching my dark mood, the better to mingle into the night I'll be driving through.

I glom onto the way everyone's always tried to keep me from answering phones all those years I couldn't stay on the wagon, even when I was cocooned with the wife during the "good" times. Phones would only bring me trouble, white lines of blow stretching from the outside world to my nose, and then my veins. I had to get beyond a diet of Grand Marnier and iron-cooked minute steaks.

There's no traffic as I roll north, babbling on in my head. I turn on the radio and find just enough bandwidth to keep me feeling connected, as though I needed to make a path by which to escape my inner self's whistling roar. To listen to the songs of others, and not just my own, written or not.

One station's running news about some lady becoming president of the Philippines, how the Marcoses were forced to flee by dark of night. Were they holing up in Quality Inns now, like me? There's a recall on over-the-counter capsules ever since one was found laced with cyanide. We're on the verge of war with Libya, but also making noise about Iran getting nukes. A senator named Kerry's going on about secret drug funding of right-wing militias to counter the Soviets. How we're also backing insurgents in Afghanistan.

I fiddle the dials. Sick of sports news. Stop for a power ballad. I hum along, then go full-throated as best I can...old driving trick. Maybe a route back to creativity?

"Why'm I so bad to you, something I never wanted to do," I write. The sky darkens and I drive north into the heart of Dixie. "We used to dance. A different circumstance."

Not bad.

If I'd been a crying man, I'd have tears streaming down my face. There's a song on the radio all about agin,' losing one's looks.

I try to get an image of my kid, *my* boy, into my head. I catch the rearview, the look of my tired eyes staring back at me quizzically, as though wondering what in tarnation I'm up to now.

That old dwarf-guy Cato sure as shit rattled me. After he disappeared into the glare of that Winter Park motel lot light, the whole rest of the afternoon had had that same foggy feeling I'd started with coming out of the shower, as though I could never clear the mirror enough to see straight. As though everything had blurred into one eternal blackout, like the bad times before detox, or the guilt of the first few weeks back on, after falling.

"Bad as an omen," I say out loud. I shudder, recalling my lifelong fear of the shower curtain plastering itself upside my skin like the specter of death.

I just hope Junior isn't hurt. I remember the tragic feeling we all had when Robert Plant lost *his* kid.

Things were sure as hell funny when they happened to me, from pitchforks in the foot to motorcycles off bridges. But when others got hurt, comedy slipped to tragedy. Could this be my paternal streak returning? A lost glimmering of soul I'd never thought possible to find again? That look in *my* Pa's eyes transferred, somehow, into my own?

I remember back to when everyone started dying that summer of 1970. Jimi and Janis. The trio of ODs that hit Bearsville in the Spring of '73, moving so many of us in the music community back out of town for a second round in California. And then more death, way out there, moving us back to the land of snow and mountains, a few seasons later.

There's a strange disconnect to everything. I never could find the keys to my room. Rented this car, somehow, without any paperwork I can remember. Rang the bell in the motel lobby endlessly with no one answering. Seemed to be able to see all the rest of the band, the roadies, and our manager, all grouped together, heads down, inside the Lounge when I stopped by there to tell them what was happening, how I had to head north. Then the windows fogged up.

I just split.

You know how it is when you get so crowded in the head that everything starts to sound and feel like static? And not a young man's fuzziness, but something older, with layers of responsibilities and regrets all kicking at what's right in front of you so that it becomes hard to even speak or listen, let alone take in what it is that is real and alive all around you.

Looking through that cloudy picture window into the Cheek to Cheek lounge, what I saw felt like some other man's dream. Levon, with that way he'd gotten since he first acted in movies, had this poker-straight posture in his legs and neck while trying to seem relaxed in his back and butt. Only the tautness in his clean-shaven jaw signaled the fear he'd taught his angry eyes to hide. He was only looking up when addressed, as if something was eating at him. Rick, rubber-legged and scruffy-drunk as usual, strode about behind everyone, slapping at his arms as though trying to wake himself. The roadies all huddled together on a couch. Joe, our new manager, sat on the edge of his easy chair gesticulating, lecturing, a slew of paperwork laid out in front of him. Big-boned and bearded, shirt un-tucked and looking like he could use a drink. Letters? Forms and such? It was too misty to tell. Garth, as always, seemed to be asleep on another couch, laid out with his hands on his chest like some stone knight in a museum. His zip-up boots, forlorn, stood up neatly next to the same coffee table on which Joe's papers sat.

Worse were the calls I put in later to Liz and Junior. Someone would answer. I could hear them talking, asking if there was anyone on the line. But they couldn't hear *my* answers, *my* entreaties, *my* questions about what was going on. Same happened when I tried getting numbers for the police, for anyone up in Woodstock. I could hear them, plain as song, but they couldn't hear me, even when I yelled. Even when I tried singing.

I found myself feeling the clamshell-sand of a Florida parking lot under foot as though I were wearing nothing but socks. Even though I had boots on. And even with the sun on me, I felt chill. The air didn't seem to be moving even though I could see and hear palms rustling all around. The traffic passed me by without sound.

With the world now going from purple to black around me, headed north on 301, I can taste a mixture of salt, sulfur, and chlorine at the back of my mouth, like beach town water. Feel sand in my bathing suit even though I'm wearing knit pants and a tight silk shirt and haven't been to the shore in a decade. Sense that I'm forgetting something, the way you do when you're a kid trying to understand what adults are talking about. Or are in some foreign country, listening in on the conversation at the next table. It's all a foreign tongue, bub.

It pisses me off that I can't quite get some things. Like all this aging crap. That old man version of me I keep catching in the rearview every time I look for my son's eyes in mine. The mist in the motel room. My whole fucking life shot all to shit without my being able to do anything about it, like having to force the nice dreams to end before you piss yourself in bed. It's an ungodly struggle.

I'm lost on the FM dial. Madonna's *Crazy for You* sears into my brain.

"Smoky air. The weight of my stare." I write on my scribble pad after I switch the radio off so I can listen to the whoosh of radials on asphalt. "So close yet far away."

I flash back on a hellish morning and the sleepy sounds the tires were making as I rolled my Mustang down the hill from 101 into the Malibu Beach Colony, thinking I'd get away with not waking Liz and the kid one too many mornings. Lipstick on the collar, the rim of my man panties. She, the dear wifey, had told me just the week before—after she'd heard that Mickey Twist had moved in down the street—that I was breaking the camel's back.

I'd been out with Eric, Harry, and the crazy Brit boys Johnny and Mr. Moon. Mr. Twist had told me my time was up before it all started. Said I was on the slide now and would have to pay the piper. Or find him new clients. Keith, Mickey said, just wasn't reliable enough. I should go out and find someone younger. Maybe stretch the wings beyond rock and roll and find one of those up-and-coming actors just coming up like a flock of phoenixes shot out of the flames of our own decades-long burnout.

Someone, not sure who, turned blue that night. The moon-man smacked up a car. Twist got to talking up the film crowd Robbie had started bringing 'round the studio, mentioning on the side that they'd likely be his future.

Somehow, I got in just before dawn, certain that all would be well, and mom and dad would never know for the worse. But then I decided the family needed a good breakfast. And not just coffee and toast, but bacon and eggs and pancakes and muffins... the whole lot.

"You set my goddamned kitchen on fire," Liz said, standing in the doorway as Moonie and I sat on the floor playing hot potato with flaming toast, unaware of the blazing drapery behind us, or the fire alarm loudly sounding. "You bastard. I told you one last straw and here you are. Fuck you, Richard."

"Seems the missus is missing something," Moon said with a leering wink.

That's when hell happened on us in all its fury. In the sweetest package, of course.

Junior, still in diapers, waddled in from the open front door with a piece of paper in his hand. He handed it to his mother.

"Where's Richard?" was all it read. That was enough.

I felt like crying.

I could hear Twist's diesel Mercedes purring outside.

Here on 301, I turn the radio back on. Afraid of my own thoughts, my memories.

That last straw played out ten years past. Maybe, if I tried the AM dial, I'd find one of those stations like WLAC in Nashville, which broadcast thousands of miles north to my mechanic dad's house on the maple-shaded street we lived on in Stratford. Or Cleveland's WJW, Toronto's CIVT. They'd corrupted all I was learning in the Baptist Church Choir as effectively as that bitch piano teacher who slammed away my ability to read music as sure as she smashed my fingers. All because I added my own notes to the tunes. If I wanted to be original, she told me, as tears streamed my teen-pimpled face, be a composer.

My parents said the same thing. My women...Liz and now Dawn, who spent the last month on this kick about me being too this and that. Too needy. Too pushy. Too controlling. Too submissive. Too talkative. Too quiet. Too much in my damned head.

Crazy mama's boy. Drowning every sorrow that ever passed your way, seeking out comfort from someone new every day.

I find a station, scratchy but loud, that's playing all the guys who got me going in the beginning. They're countdowning to the new Rock and Roll Hall of Fame inductions. Chuck Berry, Fats Domino, the Everly Brothers, Buddy Holly, Jerry Lee Lewis, and Elvis Presley were already in. Our kind of music, along with my master, Mr. Ray Charles. But none of that other inductee, the Godfather of Soul. Hey, we weren't in his neck of Georgia yet. Coming up: Aretha, Muddy, Marvin, Roy Orbison, Smokey Robinson. The Coasters.

I pull into a Shell station to get gas. A lanky, chicken-necked kid with no shirt and a bad sunburn ambles up to the car and stands by the window. It's like I see him coming but don't realize he's real. When he taps on the window I near jump out of my skin. I motion for him to fill it, not talking for some reason. When he's done, I go to pass him my American Express card, but he just stares at it through the glass, slowly shaking his head. He motions that I should just drive on.

Not one to question opportunity, I pull back onto the highway. The radio turns to static halfway through *Heartbreak Hotel* and I think I hear bells, or at least the kind of sound a car makes when its lights are left on, or a door gets opened.

Must be having flashbacks, I think. There's this craggy guy in the back seat, the spitting image of Vincent Price. He's wearing a giant white cowboy hat, holding a golden statue of a man figure in his hand. I take it in stride. Ghosts don't scare me. Only the living who want to make a ghost out of me. Best bet's to engage the specter. Fast.

"That dude Cato was something else," I say. "I'd have thought to ask someone whether this journey was indeed necessary if it weren't that I somehow know it is. The way you just know things sometimes."

I glance into the rearview and Vincent's looking at the gold man in his hand, rubbing its head like some sacred talisman.

"I just want a sense of assuredness again. Like the feel of the wheel on my fingers or the subtle pressure from the accelerator under my foot, the way one touches the brakes ever so lightly to see if they're still there," I go on, doing as I say when I say it. "Signs of life, or maybe just that notion of forward motion."

The car lurches, swerves slightly when I play the wheel. Still no response from the guy in the back seat.

"Surety doesn't always have to be good to make sense. It just has to be there, like that glimpse of how one really looks, or the sound of one's own voice on a tape machine or recording. Hell, I had it best, probably, that time I just knew, like a cold shower, that it was over, once and for all, between Liz and me after Mickey's visit," I yap on, catching glimpses of my passenger as I hurtle northwards, his face eerily lit from below. "Malibu, again; that unreal world with the ocean on the wrong side. Soon after Moonie near drowned in those surfer waves, mixing yellow jackets and Martell. You know it was the record company that hired Twist to be my 'handler,' in charge of keeping me creative, as they say."

I go silent. I've stumbled onto another painful part of my story. So what if the guy in back's not even there? Some things just can't be said aloud.

Liz kept repeating that line about me having drawn my last straw as she packed her bags and gathered the kid and his gear into the car, screaming and staring me down like I was some hand-in-the-cookie-jar criminal. I was a bad, bad daddy. An even worse husband.

What can I say to this silent guy in the back seat? That I never felt more alive than I did that morning, feeling not only the fabric, but the inner feathers of the down pillows I hugged there in our driveway in the early morning California sun as she pulled away and was gone? So what if I'd passed out? The kitchen fire hadn't been bad enough to hurt anyone. Royalty checks were still coming in. I still sang *You Don't Know Me* for her whenever times got bad, just as I'd first wooed her with the same chestnut back when we were but kids.

If only I could just drive this long highway, this darkening 301, up and out of Georgia to that moment and right it. With a song.

"Ever get sick of aging?" I ask. "I'm worried about my kid, what my life may have done to him."

No answer. The guy's looking out the window into the deepened darkness. I roll down the window. The rush of cooling March air against my arm, through the shirt and jacket, its fast rustle through my beard and hair, feels good.

The old guy, seen in my rearview, has put a hand onto his hat to keep it still. He's still looking to the side. I join him and watch the kudzu whiz by and before long we cross some border and see the first signs for Statesboro.

Last time I'd spent real time down here in peach country was when we recorded a song for Carter's campaign. It was all we could do, I told the rest of the boys, since none of us could vote. As a thank you, the governor invited us all down to Plains, where we

blew a joint in the limo riding through peanut fields to sit at Ms.
Rosalyn's breakfast table eating up her soft-scrambled eggs and his
cheesy grits. I cracked them both up good wiggling my eyebrows
and using my best growling cornpone take on southern reactions
whenever she asked what a nice Canadian boy like me had been
doing in Arkansas.

I look into the darkness of the back seat when a car comes toward
us. Now the guy's looking straight ahead, though still not meeting
my eyes in the rearview. He looks familiar, like an older version of
someone I've been close to but am trying to forget and remember
at the same time; like someone my mind has made older out of
spite. I catch my own gaze momentarily and start speaking again.

"I started with the best when I wrote. Smoothed out a few things
that were handed me and then all downhill from there. Always
the pressure to top myself," I say. "And meanwhile, caught behind
the piano, off to the side, everyone else took to shimmying in the
spotlight as though they were the real stars. Maybe some emotions
just can't be shared, especially when they up and combine, deep
inside, with the knowledge that you simply aren't worth much.
Like, hasn't it all been done before?"

We pass through a small town; street lamps light my passenger
again. This time I catch the guy glaring at me like some angered
gnome, as though I'd just insulted his mother.

"When you get pulled, you go," I hear a rumbling, movie-twang
voice say, even though the guy's lips don't seem to be moving in
the shifting light. "When you're going, you figure out just what it
is that's pulling you, my friend. Climb your mountain, daddy-o."

I swear I hear the car's donging door sound again and shudder
up my spine. The radio comes back on to static even though I'm
sure I'd turned it off miles before. The man in the white hat's gone.

I realize it's been a day since I've eaten. I spot a roadside tavern and pull in. One of those in-between places I still dream about, remembered from my long-ago days on the road when we were all fresh out of high school and keen for overpowering anything that came before us that looked, remotely, like an audience.

There are beer lights in the saloon window, and a sandy parking lot paved with shiny, squashed-flat bottle tops. A whole mess of pick-ups and giant bruiser cars of decent vintage, rusting away in the blinking light of a sign announcing Pulled Pork BBQ and Live Band Tonight!

I park between a Camaro and a battered Mercury convertible with DC plates. It feels good to stretch a bit when I get out of the car. March air, at least in Georgia, feels like August in the Catskills, minus the bugs.

My throat feels raw, like my whole neck's been stretched some strange way. Thirst, I figure.

I'm not used to pondering so much, worrying over things I should have spent time worrying about long ago. Haven't taken any long drives this sober in a long time, either. The road, for me, has always been about sleeping, be it naturally or with eyes open, the memory shut off through whatever means.

I'm ready to get back to some sort of flow. I'm sick of all this strangeness. I want to find a pay phone and try calling Woodstock again, seeing what's up, maybe calm my worst fears.

Sure as shit, times feel good the moment I open that saloon's swinging doors and get hit by the second chorus of the great Doctor Ray's *Lonely Avenue,* along with a whole mess of beer and bourbon-scented menthol cigarette smoke. The song's being sung by an old black dude in a purple suit and tinted aviator glasses, backed on the small bandstand by a group of bored-looking white kids with scraggly long hair and wispy beards.

The old guy's giving the song his heart with his whole body swaying, Ray-like, to the pulse of Charles' deeply rhythmic song. "I'm crying, I'm crying, I'm crying..." the white kids sing to him at the break as he wails back about living his life lonely.

It's like I've come home. Or maybe, as I'm starting to think too often, I've up and died. Gone to some sort of rock and roll heaven.

I order myself some pulled pork and beer, thinking about how nice it'd be if this type of food caught on elsewhere one day. I take that first, spine-chillingly good sip of an icy mug of brew as the song ends and I hear mumbling from the bandstand.

"For our latest friend to join us here in this den of the excommunicated," says the dude on stage, looking my direction. "For all of us here on the fringes of this world we still call soul..."

With one note on his keyboard, I know the guy's into another of my Ray faves, even before he starts ratcheting his baritone up into a high falsetto like I was once able to do.

"Aww-ooh, Georgia," he intones, eyes alighting somewhere on the wall further off, above and beyond me.

The room erupts and before I know it, I'm hitting those high notes with him. Even without another hit of beer.

4

Wheels of a Delta 88 spin fast on winter-ravaged Upstate roadways. Fallow fields, half-encrusted in snow, the rest furrowed in frozen field-rot and iced-over mud, unfurl themselves on either side of a moonlit ridge. Spent barns bending under a zillion stars. Homey, yellow dash lights and a large speedometer with its needle moving quickly right, then left. The lemon moon waning.

Klokko heading east into the Catskills terrain he'd known since he was a boy riding in the backseat, pretending to be asleep as his dad, all grunts and groans, negated everything his Ma said.

His younger brother, Gerard, took the place of Pa in Ma's eyes. He always gave her what she wanted, what she needed, until he left the picture too early. Far too early.

There was a comfort to this landscape, especially in the dark when it matched his dreams, and not just his guilt at never having measured up.

The Oldsmobile purred through sleeping hamlets and villages lit by scattered streetlamps dimmed by dead bugs, ringed with winter's dirt crust. Klokko made sure to stick within the speed limit...on the upper side.

The stiff-necked, rail-thin, scraggly-bearded driver took in all he passed. Empty storefronts, boarded-up boarding houses with scattered appliances on multiple porches. Street lots centered by corrugated metal storage sheds and dark homes, some asbestos or vinyl-sided, some peeling paint and emitting the flickering blue light of unwatched late night television talk shows. The occasional brightly lit soda pop machine or convenience store. Dying fluorescents skittering their way back to black. The sad, endless look of late winter/early spring on the edge of the Catskills.

Klokko ejected the *Big Pink* tape he'd been playing for days and surrounded himself with strumming guitars and harmonized male voices. The Everly Brothers on lush 8-track; *Let It Be Me* split into halves, connected by a whirr and a click and another whirr. Accompanied, always, by this great fan's breath-singing—whistles and hums and an occasional word or two at a half-pace behind the song.

On the passenger side of the wide, blanketed front seat was an apple crate of worn tapes. Grateful Deads and solo Garcias, Beatles and Beach Boys, Creedence and Elvis and Roy Orbison, even Frank Sinatra. Sicilian folk songs Klokko could only phonetically mouth the words to; strange ten-cents-a-shot jazz tapes without covers. He cranked the music high and pushed the bass tones, the treble.

The whiteness of the road's edge lit swatches of forest cut into by modular homesteading. Old lawn ornaments and picnic tables; battered, front-less mailboxes of all ages and dentedness. An endless rope of sagging, pole-hung telephone and electric wires echoing the center white and yellow lines' straights, dots, and dashes.

Klokko, back in his normal driving mind, flashed back to other journeys at other ages and times. Gerard in the front seat between Ma and Pa on night drives home from his mom's uncle's farm up in Washington County, Klokko stretched out on the back seat under the blanket he now sat on, watching the night sky stay steady above the car, above the entire world they passed through fast and fleetingly.

All dead now, except Pa. He of the big house, of the flickering blue light he'd sit in front of all seasons. The father who never talked except through a locked door...or in grunts and groans. The occasional bellowed anger. Or echoing, in Klokko's head, from wherever he might have gone after he left. After Ma's passing.

There had been many Sunday drives to Albany for medical treatments. They'd pull into an A&W for frosted mugs of spicy-sweet root beer and, if Pa was in a good mood or Ma felt strong enough to speak up on Klokko and Gerard's behalf, soft-style iced custard. The two boys would sit in back competitively punching each other in arms and legs until a parent would reach back swatting, or a front seat argument broke forth.

After Gerard got himself killed, Klokko got the front seat the eight months before Ma's death. After that, Pa took him a few times to the hovels of drinking buddies or up by the spent farm in Mt. Calvary where he'd grown up.

They moved up there after closing the family house down in the village. Klokko in the back again. Silence filling the old car's interior like a thick mist.

Klokko passed the time, during those drives or when left at home, with counting. Wishing, yearning games that used the cracks in roadways, the alphabet letters in directional signs and advertisements, cows and sheep and front-yard chickens, the patterns on peeling wallpaper and the floor's cracked linoleum, alongside his own limited way with numbers. A cracked barn equaled Uncle Artie's farm; three sevens and his mother and brother ended up in heaven. He imagined the happiness of blue-lit homes in small towns; watched kids playing on tire swings, walking with bent twig fishing poles down back roads, sliding down long edge-of-town fields on runner sleds or trash can lids. If at home, he'd remember his imaginings from the road.

When Gerard started school, Klokko remembered, his brother had opened a book once while seated up front next to Pa and Pa slammed it out of his hands. The car had swerved toward an approaching station wagon, then almost hit an already battered mailbox. Gerard started crying and Klokko, remembering the salt of his memory if not the reasoning, bawled too as their father stopped the car and took to swatting the two of them, took to hitting at the seat cover, the books scattered around inside and outside the car. Eventually, Klokko couldn't remember how, Pa was out of the car hitting and kicking at fenders and tires, mouth cursing silently, no sound to be heard but Klokko's and Gerard's sobs, gasps for air, sniffles.

Breathe in, breathe out.

Ma went away to tend her own mother's illness, which eventually ended when she passed after a couple months. That car, a giant mustard-green Ford marked by the growing rust spots where Dad had laid into it, went up into the back meadow at his grandparents' empty farm. There'd been another vehicle between it and this Olds, a yellow Buick his Ma had gotten from her father when he grew too sick to drive. But Pa wrecked that one into a tree after she died; he'd had it towed, too, to Mt. Calvary when he moved there. Field furniture.

Klokko thought about shooing lumbering skunks and scampering raccoons from the peeling rooms there. The old, gnarled tree
under which Gerard was buried. And Ma. He never saw anything
from his previous village life again, except for the Ford up in the
back meadow, and his mother's traveling blanket, saved from his
father's frequent cleaning-outs. He'd placed it between his box
spring and mattress in the musty-smelling room that was now his
own hovel with the cracked windows covered in cardboard.

The moon rolled up over a distant hill, backlighting road signs
and telephone poles and distant trees in a hollow.

That red-headed young woman in the house by Sid's Ford, his
beloved; she had looked into his soul, made his head spin. Klokko
thought there is a God in my gut, a God on these roads, in this
interminable waiting and hoping and yearning. Events and memories and sadnesses mount, one atop each other, like a house made
of strong bricks. Fire-proof. There is and was and always will be a
meaning in all things. It matters not whether one creates or simply
appreciates the stuff of life. You wait. It is the way of knights,
of those with nothing but chivalrous good in their veins. Mom
and Gerard smile down from heaven, give meaning to everything
they see just as others like them, ghosts on the night roads of our
sprawling, dying counties and towns, smile down on everyone, on
everything. Time returns, Klokko thought. Pa will surface some
day and actually speak after all these years, and he will let me back
into his own father's, grand-dad's, and grandmama's home. Pa will
explain why he left, say it was true what Klokko thought about him
moving south to Florida to start anew and rid himself of demons.
And Ma would tuck him in and dry away all tears. He'd find that
old book that'd been wilting for decades in the gully by County
Route 3 or wherever it was Pa threw it. The one Gerard had been

reading, about knights and heroes and gallant returns. The dead could and would return. They would because they could. Life did continue. On its own.

Klokko turned off the headlights and whooshed on through the ice-edged, equinox-approaching night in the direction of the slow-rolling lemon moon, careening down rural backroads with the force of all memory, hope, and yearning pushing him onward. He latched onto the idea of his Pa smiling once more, seated in some lounge in some place near the Disney World.

Should he U-turn back home or sit the night out at Sid's Ford? He could wait for the dawn light to strike his beloved lady's windows, to climb across her far wall and kiss her sweet eyes awake. He could then open his car door as she opened her front door on that porch he knew so well. Could watch, lovingly, as she stepped out onto the road without looking in either direction to come to his long-closed, now-open arms to say, if only with eyes and spirit and heart, "It's alright. Come to me, now, as I've come to you. The time's ours, dear. It's our time."

Klokko thought of all those songs that are so good you can't help but stop them halfway through to start them all over again to hear them better, to not miss any of it with one's meandering mind. Those ghost voices that sing along with certain bands, sucking your soul into the music like aliens taking over your body while you sleep, leaving no memory of dreams when you awake. There was a holiness in the world he'd learned to hear in rock and roll, taught himself to see in the landscape he'd grown up in. It was the same beautiful sighing sadness that he'd seen in Jesus' and Mary's faces back in those days when he still felt comfortable going to churches, when Ma was alive.

Apart from attempts by Ma to get him and Gerard to Sunday School before Pa squelched such nonsense, Klokko's experiences with religion had been spurious, at best. He joined the Methodist Church in the village when he had a crush on a Methodist girl, and later went to a Baptist revival meeting in a big metal pole barn outside the county seat because another girl he lusted after during junior high, her ears peeking out from long straight auburn hair, had said she'd like it if he went with her. After two days of holding her hand as the preacher talked damnation, he fled. Later, he tried his hand at the Catholic Church, on the hill dotted with burned homes outside of town, drawn by the dark-eyed Italian beauties he imagined going there. Loved the pomp and circumstance, the ceremony and smells and endless music. The way smoke played in the shafts of light spilling down from on high. But in the end, he felt embarrassed when asked to step out of the line for those going onto their knees before a burnished rail to be given thin white wafers and tastes of wine.

Had he been baptized?

He couldn't lie, then or now.

The first time Klokko saw the lady he now loved; she was standing on her parents' porch yelling back inside through an open door. And he'd immediately thought of running up to that rail, paint-peeled instead of burnished, to beg communion from her. It was late autumn, Halloween decorations still hanging on trees. She was but a girl, knock-kneed and gawky-eyed with straight bangs and a colt-like gait. He couldn't, and wouldn't if his life depended on it, explain why he found her attractive. It was just so. Same as in the great stories of the Round Table, of Roland and Lancelot and Abelard.

She, his beloved, was everything the Everlys were singing about. The Beatles. Van and Neil. All the love songs and none of the meaner, Stones-type or Dylanesque women. Those sneering rockers were for the sort he saw staring at him from the naked pictures in magazines, or the teasers who lined the halls in high school. All who gave him mean looks. Or acted as though he had cooties, from grade school on into adulthood. That harder music was for love gone wrong, for channeling the anger he knew he had taken with him from Pa. From the specter of death that had landed on his family.

She in the window, in the flowered nightie and flowery room, hadn't done any of that mean stuff to anyone yet. And wouldn't if he could just be good and quiet enough about what he was feeling.

Klokko loved her so much he didn't give her a name. She'd tell him what it was when the time came. And whatever it was would be better for coming from her lips, and not his imagination. He knew this like faith.

Klokko had been called Richie once. His mother had called him Her Darling. His Pa never really said much except to tell him, after Gerard and Ma passed on, that he'd heard from the guys down at the station that everyone had been calling him Klokko for years.

Klokko didn't even think to ask why. He knew the story. He'd been a blusher. And not only that, a dreamer. He was always having crushes. His blushes and facial tics gave it away.

"Richie's got a thing for Sally May," Gordon Mason chanted. Larry Smith caught him going beet red, his mouth a drawling exclamation point, when Deborah Campbell brushed by his seat just before recess. "Richie's gone all red. Look at his mouth. He's got a clock face," Donnie Malloy blurted out. Fourth grade. "Richie's a clock-o. Richie's a clock-o."

The term stuck, was written on the bathroom walls in ninth grade, with Ks.

No one called Klokko Richie anymore. Not even he, himself. Only when he dreamed of the girl with the reddish blonde hair in the upstairs room with the soft yellow light, with the cat he wished he were, nested in her lap. Only then did Klokko imagine ever being Richie again.

Somewhere behind him, a car crested the hill as he drove, lightless. He turned his own beams back on. A cluster of mobile homes appeared to his left, a plywood school bus stop to the right. A faint orange glow emanated from behind a hill. He knew this town, knew that in its center was an all-night gas station, nestled into a corner, where someone would say "hi" and nod matter-of-factly in his direction. He still had a twenty in his pocket; enough to fill the car back up and leave some change for later. Klokko tensed, quickly freeing his mind for the torment of neon lights, of other people. He had lived here way back when.

The lot was empty as he pulled up to fuel the 88. Placing his gas cap into the nozzle to free his hands, Klokko grabbed a squeegee and cleaned his windows before a freeze started in. He checked out the windows of the convenience store. A clerk was watching something, probably a TV, above the door. Klokko tensed, finished his windows, topped off the tank.

The wind picked up. The moon moved behind a cloud, darkening the world around the canopy of lights.

Klokko darted to the store, threw open the door and slapped his bill on the counter as the station clerk turned his direction. It was one of the high school crowd who had named him Klokko some twenty years earlier.

When he got in his car a second later, he thought of letting out a yell of relief. But as usual, he stifled himself. Just like his Pa had always made him do. Hold the crying, boy, he'd say. Hold it all in or there'll be Hell to pay.

Klokko revved his engine and pulled back out onto the road, peeling through the small-town streets clustered around the little-used crossroads, until he pulled into the parking lot by the Central School. He settled in behind some parked busses where he'd go unnoticed.

Adrenaline pushed his mind awake. Klokko liked being hidden in the cocoon of his car; he lived for the endless music he could play as a soundtrack to his thoughts, as if there were some cogent narrative to the push and pull of his emotions and how they shaped his life.

I want my own memories now, Pa, Klokko muttered while putting a new 8-track in the player. I want my own story, finally. I'll find you, man. I'll set myself free, he said. He headed back into his night. Didn't Pa realize that Klokko had to run as he had? It was in the blood.

All around him surged the sound of The Band's *Music from Big Pink*, and his soul's doppelganger, Richard Manuel, singing about his own father, his own tears of rage.

5

The singer knows me. We played the same circuits when practically all of us were getting pegged by someone or other as the next big thing, the music's rising star. Jerry Washington. Used to sing with Otis and, before him, played organ in one of Little Richard's touring bands.

"You don't need credentials, man. Your version of Georgia was credentializing enough for me," I tell him after he comes over to my table. "It's just good to be talking to somebody. Been in the car too long. You know where it's at."

Washington's standing tall over me, rocking a bit on his battered black cowboy boots, eyes lost beneath shades.

"So, what happened?" I ask, voice phlegmy from disuse. "What you doing playing behind an anonymous Live Band Tonight sign in some backroads nightspot off 301? I mean, I thought I was scraping bottom touring places with four-fifths of my old band..."

"My man," Washington replies, pulling up a chair and motioning the waitress away as she approaches. "Sometimes you just do things wrong without knowing it. Play a bit too loose at the pool table. Get a bad boilermaker. Chase after the wrong skirt and mess up everything you once thought was righter than right."

He tells a story about how he'd been leading this band about to get a recording contract back when the whole R&B/soul thing shifted to funk. Had a wife and two kids but figured he had to dive whole hog into the wide-lapel, mighty bell-bottom, high-afro look. Snorted several shares of coke. Before he could say "back-atcha," Jerry Washington tells me, he'd lost it all, the contract, the marriage. Ended up in the hospital with a minor heart attack. Got intervened into rehab. Joined the church, same as Solomon Burke and his old boss, Little Richard. But then got caught cursing out a heckler and was excommunicated.

"Which is how we done got our name here," he chuckles. "So, what brings you through looking so dead-awful yourself?"

I start to tell him all about how me and the boys had gotten back together, despite critics' warnings, so we could make a bit of extra dough before the chance disappeared. I'd needed something to get me out of my own wicked ways, I add with a wink. I'd tried solo gigs but wanted a bit more of the past.

"I endanger myself when I don't have the work," I say, motioning Jerry to sit down. "I mean, it's one thing to be ambitious, another to have made it. Next thing you know you've reached a point where you go and puke in the damned gutter and everybody calls that brilliance personified. Hear that long enough, you start to think they're right and puke up more and more. You call it art."

Washington nods his big, graying head and takes off his shades, rubs his eyes as he starts to speak.

"I hear you, brother. You get to a point where no one hears the mistakes anymore. You stop growing," he says, looking down at the table. "At least in holes like this you find someone each night who's got no choice but to listen."

For some reason, I start telling this man I haven't seen in 20 years all about the strange little man who'd come to my motel room to tell me about Junior, how I felt compelled to do my fatherly duty even though I hardly knew my own kid and hadn't been able to get through to anyone to confirm what might have happened. I even tell him a bit about Dawn and how he might have seen pictures of her in the gossip pages back when she used to get around. I want to tell him about the fog in the bathroom, the strange apparition in the car, but he stops me when I utter Dawn's name.

"The looker?" he asks.

"Yeah," I reply. "And the papers never ran no pictures of her ass."

I hold off telling him about my marriage, the lost years. After all, this is a rhythm and blues joint, not given to the deep field hollering type of blues my story would need. And what was to tell, anyway? That ever since those early days, playing spots just like this while still in my teens, I'd made two lives for myself. One, me the cut-up, always hitting it a bit harder than the rest, while the other was Mr. Sensitive, cooing over that single woman out beyond the stage lights who could have been my Ma, up on some pedestal. Isn't it always so?

I take a sip of beer and shut my eyes, flashing on the two me's, one shaved and broody-eyed, crooning inches from the microphone while eyeing everyone in the crowd. Pointy shoes and silk shirts at book parties, art openings, and Hollywood shindigs. Then that other me, shaggy bearded, making faces and acting all scarecrow like, telling stories about misadventures and bad dreams. The Goofy I joked with Junior about. Some weirdo middle-aged, sad-sack Upstate guy.

Eyes open, half-hearing Jerry Washington talk about spending most of his time in this neck of the woods now, semi-retired he called it, I catch a glimpse of me living again in that wintry Woodstock I'm now headed to. What it was to hold a newborn, watch the snow fall. Isn't that where the beard first came in? Watching TV in my socks, sobering up. Getting my act together.

Only later did I need that drink or three before the performances the boys talked me into, so I wouldn't seem so damned depressed.

Could it have been some circle, all this?

I snap to as Washington segues into a story about how he ended up having to spend time in the same penitentiary James Brown had once been sent to. I feel bad I've not been listening, though he doesn't seem to mind. When he hits a pause, I let him know I'm there with him.

"Good story, man. Sad, but that's the way life works," I say. "You know, I got woke up this morning by the weirdest old coot, man. Just got out the shower and he's standing in my doorway like some avenging angel of light telling me to go climb some friggin' mountain."

Jerry's looking towards the stage as his band of young white guys signal they're ready for the next set. One of the guitarists squats next to an amp, re-tuning. The drummer hits a few beats, practices a roll, hits the bass pedal a couple times. The sparse crowd is talking louder, the way drinkers do as the night rolls on. The place is hazy with smoke.

"Something's up and I don't know what it is," I continue as Jerry rises from his seat. "It's like I can't read the story of my life anymore. All the peaks and pits are flattening out. I feel I'm stuck in some time capsule, like I'm being pegged to fill some sad slot. Yet I've also got this weird speedy feeling going on like I've been bailed out of jail. It's like I'm shifting from being an active to a passive player in my own drama. Or maybe it's the other way around. I dunno..."

"Dude, follow the mystery," Washington replies, distracted. "Lounges are lounges. Go where you're needed. Write your own book. Make each song count like it's your own."

The big man flashes me his classic showman's smile.

"Can we catch up on this road trip of yours after I play a few? These white boys get restless but fast, man," Jerry Washington says with a wink. "And you do know how much we'd love it if you came up and sang one with me. Besides, I got something you need to see when we get our next break."

I beg off with a cough and some fluttering of my hands. Jerry says he knows how it is as he lumbers off. He orders me a pitcher before getting back up on stage. Plus, a full tumbler of Grand Marnier.

Mr. Washington and The Excommunicated start in on a loping, gator-rock version of *I'm Your Puppet.*

Lizzie's the love of my life. I think back to when she was a model. Cute, brunette, and carry-around-the-room petite with a ballet dancer's training to boot. Warm puppy dog eyes and an upward lilt to the ends of her sentences, singsong as a bird. Born and raised, until six, in some fairytale Scandinavian city. Started working at 16, showing cars in a Chevrolet showroom. Some advertising Svengali re-arranged her into the beauty I first met on Yonge Street in swinging sixties Toronto, all Twiggy-eyed in a leg-enhancing skirt suit.

When she came into the Friar's Tavern that winter of '64 with her fellow models, how could I NOT notice? Hell, I almost lost my way through Ray's *He Don't Love You.* I still recall to this oddest of days, which note she came into my life on. It's where my voice cracks each time I sing it. Hell, it's *why* I still sing that one.

Some genius should chart all great performances back to such moments. We're predictable, after a fashion. Our hurts are fuel. Our art's nothing but fire.

Liz called me her Hamlet. "You're Rock's great tragic figure," she'd say, taking it further than the fact that I'd come from a town called Stratford, near a muddy Canadian flatlands river called the Avon. "The Prince in waiting, but more than any Hal," I'd always reply.

I sang *Please, Please, Please*. Got the band to follow me into *How Sweet It Is* and *You've Really Got a Hold on Me* before Danko unplugged his bass, saying it was time for a break.

He and I moved over to her table, and all I remember are Liz's eyes, the murmur of bar noise and some Ventures tune playing on the jukebox. Now, when I recall '60s Toronto, I think only of that moment.

And then my kid. And then again, my fuck up as a father.

I take a long swallow of the Grand Marnier and hold its sticky-sweet orange kick for several seconds on the tongue. First time I tried the stuff was with her. A fancy dinner-date at the City Club, acting all kick-ass but upper-class. The drink matched my borrowed, thin-lapel jacket and the only tie I had at the time, one with a musical note just above its vee. Which in turn matched the flavor of the room we were dining in, all lake-fronting windows on one side, and shimmering mica-fronted wallboard on the other. White tablecloths. A sense that the other tables' aged folk were unable to keep their eyes off our youth.

So what if I felt the imposter, like I'd get caught for the small town hick I was? Liz laughed when I shared my fears, saying that was exactly how *she* felt *all* the time.

Grand Marnier...could its sticky sweetness, which I finished off with a couple more swallows, be the reason for this current dullness enveloping me.

Liz and I talked about having kids. Settling down. Double careers.

What happens?

Back in real time, in this roadside bar in bumfuck Georgia, I follow the hard liquor with a long draft of beer. I'm hoping to transform something, anything, within me. I lean back in my chair, tipping it as far as I can without spilling onto my back, and watch the lights from the bar, stage and jukebox play across the saloon's wide stamped-tin ceiling.

"So, you being pulled or pushed?" Washington asks. "You going to follow the action or set it rolling now?"

I startle and drop my chair back to the floor with a thud, not having noticed that his set had ended and my pitcher emptied. "You following a dream or chasing some rainbow? Fucker or fucked? Good daddy or bad son? Dead or alive, man?"

Washington seats himself and says he'd read something about me. He orders a new pitcher and Marnier for me, an iced tea for himself.

"I've heard about your new lady's type," he says low and confidential, leaning across the table and putting a meaty hand on my arm. "How you get into that ball and chain thing?"

He lets go of my arm, pushes *his* chair back, and cackles a low, end-of-the-road laugh I recall from way too many late nights on the road. It reminds me of Keith Moon's chirp, Jim Morrison's snort, Brian Jones' whiny guffaws. I want to run but chuckle along.

"You know how it is, man," I say. "It's like you win the lottery and your whole life falls apart. I...I didn't give a shit for years. About anything..."

My throat's sore. I need to soothe it. I take two alternating sips of the drinks before me.

Washington's aging face seems lit from below as he talks, punctuating each sentence, each thought, with a gleaming-eyed grin. Same as that apparition from the back seat earlier.

What's happening?

"You better call Woodstock," he says. "You never get to heaven if you don't know what road you're travelin.' I may be playing Podunk, but I done enough time in the church to know He'll be accepting me back one of these days. Once a father, always a father. And always the son."

I think of swinging my mug into Jerry Washington's face. But that's not me. Never was. I'd as soon force glass shards into my own eyes.

I want to call Junior.

"I done talked to my boys and they're wondering whether you can do that old one these white boys like so much, all about the sorry shape you're in. Drummer says he can kick ass on it. You game?"

I see my break. Feel I've spent enough time playing cat and mouse with this old friend I can't quite remember.

Washington folds his aviator glasses onto the table in front of him, rubs his eyes, and starts into some story about Otis and his final flight. The waitress is coming. I hold my hand up and he pauses. I ask where the pay phone might be, rising mid-sentence. The chair topples backwards, and all heads turn our direction.

"I'll sing it when I get off," I say as I back away. "You know how it is, man."

"You sure you're not ready to do a set with me first?" Washington asks. "Don't want you driving into any headlines tonight."

I raise my hands as if arrested, shaking my head. My set's not ready to sing.

I mumble again about making my call. My sorrow. My return.

My back's to Washington, the Excommunicated, and the bar as I swing out the saloon door into the parking lot.

"Like hell," a voice hollers.

I find a pay phone and dial Liz's number, then Joe's at the Cheek to Cheek. Same as before, I hear them but they can't hear me. I try several times, and even ring the operator. Must be the phones, I think. Damned South!

I decide to hit the road again and stumble around the parked cars, looking for something red like I usually rent.

The door opens behind me and I make to crouch behind a pickup but fall heavily onto my ass. I lean up against a big balding tire and listen as some redneck tries to make the move on his date.

"Get in the car," he slurs drunkenly. "C'mon now, jes' get in the damned car."

"I swear, I ain't never been this drunk, C.W.," comes a woman's high voice in reply. After a moment of silence, I hear a car door open and shut.

The night is alive with increasing sound. Insects, night cries, the distant rumble of traffic. I spot my car and start to crawl in its direction. Inside the bar the band starts up *Mr. Pitiful*.

I get in and sit a moment before turning the key, catching the last sweet sound of this Georgian parking lot. A strange thought hits me.

Hadn't I read, once, that Washington was dead already?

"Richard, man," I hear his basso profundo say from the back seat, this live version of Otis' classic still playing in the distance. "Didn't I tell you there was something I wanted to show you? Let's go now."

6

The Beatles 8-track started to warble. The player made a screechy sound and Klokko jumped into action. The precious *If I Fell* was being eaten.

He turned the thing off, switched his lights on, and screeched back out of the parking lot onto School Road. At the stop sign, he took a left onto 30 and, eyes darting, muscles steering, turned and sped up a gravel back hollow road. He turned the car's lights off, knowing the way like the rooms of both houses he'd lived his life in. No need to think while driving back here.

Klokko mulled his blessedness as a rock and roll fan. One holy music, many holy rock and rollers, one holy fan; that's how it was. Stuff got created. But it needed an audience as much as a start. That was his role.

He'd leave the errors of his father to the whispering wind.

Klokko switched back roads, the Olds humming between banks of snow residue. He was heading home.

Mt. Calvary was no town. Not even a hamlet. It no longer existed on maps. Just a name, like Klokko, that people had given some place that started as something else once-upon-a-time.

Mt. Calvary was made up of two things: the old, hard-bitten farm Klokko lived on and a decaying Christian camp that had long ago lost its allure. Both haunted, fallow. As forgettable and hard-forgotten as the slow-melting gravel snow. Or this fallow man approaching it in his mold-green Olds.

Klokko pulled up his gully of a driveway, edging this way and that to avoid bottoming out the Delta 88. He pulled in and stopped behind a barn and clambered across the yard to what had once been his grandpa and grandma's back door, its screen door in a heap next to where a well cover sat in another heap. His walk had a scissored, half-gait quality to it, like a man unsure whether each step will keep him moving forwards. His feet followed where they'd been before, each step fitting into the molds of previous steps in the hardened snow.

The back door creaked.

Klokko greeted the inner darkness by flicking a lighter pulled from his pocket. The orange-ish flicker dimly illuminated a cluttered kitchen, low-ceilinged, with a wood stove reconditioned for gas, 1940's ice box, rusted metal hutch, paper-crusted table, piles of canned goods and old dishes. He reached to his right and pulled forth a kerosene lamp, which he lit. As the flame adjusted, the rest of the wrecked room came into being along with his breath in the chill air.

Klokko squeezed around a gaping hole in the floor and inched forward in the direction of a strange scratchy sound. Stepped over a pile of rags and cardboard into the older interior of the house he'd made home since his mother's passing and his Pa's departure.

Back when he moved down from the barn Pa wanted him in while the two briefly shared the property.

Klokko reached down and lifted up a scraggly gray and white cat by the scruff of its neck. It purred loudly as Klokko lifted the furball to his face.

"How's my honey bun, my Beatrice?" he asked the aged critter. "Who's your loving man? Who've you been waiting to sleep the long night through with?"

He lifted the scrawny cat to his shoulder and plopped it next to his long-necked and bearded head where it sank its claws into his plaid shirt, holding on and nestling her head against his nose.

"Our lady's looking beautiful tonight, precious," he said, squeezing between a long harvest table piled high with clothes and papers and sideboards similarly festooned. The wavering lamplight lent everything an end-of-time look, like the nest a dying animal makes before it passes away. At the edges of vision, things seemed to move and scurry deeper into the mess and darkness.

Klokko and Beatrice passed a steep stairwell rendered impassable by a past cave-in. They entered a windowless room painted blood red, an old coal boiler taking up half its length with shorn-off spider-like pipes emanating from it in all directions. In the other half was a bed and a rounded kerosene heater. The place was oddly clean, every surface painted red or black. A pile of plaid shirts against the wall next to a pile of jeans. A pile of socks and an extra pair of shoes.

This was Klokko's abode.

"Beatrice, sweet pussy," he said, putting the lamp down by the bed and lifting the cat from his shoulder. "I've entered a dark time. I need to know what to do next. Shall I tell of my love? Or do I wither like the flower?"

The cat opened her mouth to let out another of her crow-like "gaaak" sounds. A wind picked up several rooms away.

Klokko lit the heater with a whoosh and stood over it until warm. Then he lay down, fully clothed, atop the bed. He put his hands behind his head, staring up at the ceiling like a daydreaming boy. His eyes settled on a mosaic of cut-out photos from magazines and newspapers. Eyes, lots of them. All framed in red and black.

"My love is nigh," said Klokko, the cat nestling onto his chest.

He put out the lamp and lay in darkness until the kerosene fire made the room glow like a heart. The light of longing.

The cat purred, then slept. Klokko stared on into his deepest thoughts. He felt his music-shrouded soul soar out over the pock-marked fields of Mt. Calvary, higher and higher until they hovered over the entire Upstate world he'd known his whole life. My soul, he was ready to bellow, is full of everlasting love. I need salvation.

"Life is like death and death releases life, but I can't understand any of it. Not love, not regret," he whispered, a hand stroking the bony cat on his chest. "I will be rewarded yet, sweet Beatrice."

Klokko tried to think what he usually thought while awaiting sleep. The look of fireflies in a field, and how they appeared to become stars as they rose into the night sky. The waterfalls he'd come to know. Their names in alphabetical and then geographic order. Buttermilk and Splish-Splash. Diamond and Horseshoe, Kaaterskill and Plattekill. Bridal Veil and Deadman Falls. He named them by height.

He would take her to all of them once she, his lady of the window across from Sid's Ford, decided it was alright to come to him. When she would call him Richie and look in his eyes and say "Yes."

Klokko loved his Catskills. When he used to read, he read about them. In Cooper's Leatherstocking Stories, or Rip Van Winkle, or that old book he would sit with at the library hour after hour until they went and locked it away in the Local History vault. The Catskill Faeries, all about little people with wings, beauties like she of the reddish blonde hair, who would secrete children away from their beds at night to visit wild and strange places. The South Seas and darkest Africa, Mayan jungles, and Arctic ice castles. The Faeries imbued each journey with Catskills fireside comfort.

It's how he traveled. Laying abed in his red room, Beatrice purring atop him. The journeys of a Klokko head.

But on this dark evening new things tugged at his mind. He'd promised his cat, and himself, that he would act on his narrative. He'd release his love. He'd find his lost Pa.

His time of action, Klokko figured.

In high school, he had discovered picture books of big land-scapes downstate towards the Hudson River. Found a novel called *Nickel Mountain* that seemed to sum it all up for a while. He looked at travel guides to see if any of them knew and loved what he knew and loved. But none of them ever did. At least the way he did.

His was an odd corner of these gently rolling but internally gnarly hills. He was off an old CCC road on the edge of the state park, within forty minutes driving time of everything that needed reaching, from the city-wise and metro-discovered little towns of Woodstock, Phoenicia, Margaretville and Roxbury to the deeper haunts of Greene County's Mountaintop, the Schoharie Valley's breadbasket, and the ornery area beyond Grand Gorge where early 19th century attempts at secession ended up in broken meetings and fist-fights amongst those trying to secede.

Klokko liked nothing better than to drive around his Catskills deep at night, playing 8-tracks as an endless sound-track to all that was in his head. Loved the music that had come out of the place, which he sometimes felt he was sprinkling back over the torn and battered terrains that had seen log-gers, tanners, quarries, hunters, farmers, gold seekers, religious zealots, and wave after wave of city-escaping weekend tourists searching for whatever it was people searched for beyond Love. Like faerie dust, this music; all those early Band songs, Jimi's quieter stuff, Tim Hardin and Tim Buckley, Dylan's homey period, NRBQ, and much of the folk music that started up at Camp Woodland before Pete Seeger got pulled east and south by the river. Arlo and Jay Ungar and so many lesser-knowns.

At times, Klokko talked with actual people about what he knew. He'd followed two photographers and a writer around. They seemed to love gabbing with him for an hour or more, the writer guy taking notes and the lady photographer asking questions and rubbing up against his arm so much he'd have to shower long in cold water when he got home to get her smell off him. The thoughts he had then weren't chivalrous or noble, Klokko knew.

He drove them around in the Olds a couple of times. Up to one of the waterfalls he loved of which they took all sorts of pictures. Over to Eminence, which had thrived in the hemlocks until some plague came through and they took down all the buildings. His three friends took notes and photos there, too.

"Why don't you show us YOUR house, man," said the male photographer in a sullen tone. Klokko said he couldn't. Not yet. And when he didn't say anything else, and blushed, they backed off.

The first time he met them he heard them talking as he fueled up the Delta 88 at a Quick Stop near DeLancey. Each of them was going non-stop, as though there weren't time to say everything each had inside. They were going on about the Catskills. Places they had seen which were the same places he had seen. Stories they had heard. Then the trio mentioned something about hobbits. Like that book his Ma had gotten out of the library to read to him. One of them, the fat reddish-haired guy, motioned in Klokko's direction with his head and the others laughed.

Hobbits, he would later think on his nightly drives. I'm a hobbit. We're all burrowing creatures up here, afraid to leave our Shire.

Later, after the woman photographer had smiled his way and the fat guy started asking him where he was from, they all sat by a fire in another old house on a hill where he heard them talking again. The woman said his name, which he'd never told her.

"He's just a clocko," she said.

"A hobbit clocko," said the fat writer.

That was the last he allowed himself to run with them. That was over a year ago.

He heard the pitter-patter of a sleety rain's beginning. March thaw. The start of changing times.

Klokko waited, head rising like a snake from the case-less pillow. Beatrice unfurled herself and stood. She made her strange gacking noise.

The two stayed silent, alert as deer. From the sounds of the roof, two stories above, they could tell what was happening. The icy shower turned into a deluge of heavier peltings. Then it quieted into snow.

"I have made a vow and like the good knight I am, Beatrice, I must cleanse myself before affecting the change I promised," he said in measured tones.

When the silent snow gave way to the clacking of ice again, Klokko stood and removed all his clothes as the cat gacked with greater, talk-like frequency. Outside, the sleet gave way to rain. Klokko sauntered through his home in ungainly nakedness to the kitchen entrance he'd entered a couple of hours earlier. The cat stayed back as Klokko opened the door to a downpour. He reached up onto a shelf for an old bar of soap and stepped hurriedly into the cold, hard rain.

Immediately soaked, Klokko walked through ice-crusted high grass past the collapsing barn and bent-over apple orchard to a small, fenced-in plot with shorn grass. He opened an old iron gate and entered a forlorn cemetery of a dozen monuments of various ages. He soaped himself and washed away the grime that had accumulated since autumn, when last the weather had been warm enough for anything but snow. Rinsed and clean, Klokko started moving his head and shoulders, first to one side and then the next, in some form of odd dance. The movement built until he was flailing around, arms akimbo like some rural Nijinsky, a deep woods performance artist of unimaginable talents.

Then, as the rain started to taper back into ice and a heavy-flaked snow, Klokko whooped, hollered, and leapt over one of the newer gravestones. His brother Gerard. He threw himself to the frozen ground and rolled like a horse in hay, a dog in goose shit. The smell of wild thyme released from under warmed snow and icy mud. He rose and leapt over a higher gravestone. Ma. Then another rubbing, this time all over, in the thyme that filled the iron fence-enclosed old cemetery and its dozen Klokko graves, thawed just enough to be fragrant when Klokko's warming flesh rubbed up against them.

By the time he was back at the kitchen door, his night vision attuned to the light of passing clouds and unveiled stars, Klokko's ancient cat stepped outside.

"Gaackk..." it implored.

"No problem, my Beatrice," Klokko replied, reaching down to pick the feline up so it wouldn't get wet or muddy from the late winter mess. He carried her to the Delta 88, where she curled up in his old blanket and purred.

"How about some old favorites," he said, carefully prying the spent Beatles' tape out with a kitchen knife, unthreading its captured portions, and wrapping it in a safe, meticulous bundle. He pulled out an 8-track of The Beach Boys from behind his visor and popped it into the player. He roared the engine to life and turned the sound on. *Pet Sounds'* harmonies filled the car's interior and he slid into gear, rolling out the driveway onto gravel. After a mile he switched some running lights on.

Klokko and Beatrice were back off Mt. Calvary. His day of promised change was before them. He sped up and breathed/sang along with the music. The cat purred.

God Only Knows, the tune. God only knows, the thought.

7

"On Sunday the Lord rose in glorious splendor. He overcame suffering and destroyed all that began with Eve's sin and was furthered by the shame of her man Adam, acquiesced to by her husband Adam," chanted a rail-thin six-foot-six man with tin foil on his head, kneeling in a cloister of trailer homes brightly painted with folk images of bearded saints and blonde-wigged angels. Multi-colored words from the bible filled every inch of metallic surface in sight. "He brought back sinners and clothed them in white robes of glory so they, too, could worship our father. How awesome is this moment!"

Jerry Washington also wore tin foil on his head, muttering along with the tall white priest.

"You have united, dear Father, dearest son, your divinity with our humanity and our humanity with your divinity; your life with our mortality and our deaths with your sense of purpose," the thin man continued.

My legs were asleep, thwarting my impulse to bolt.

"You have assumed what is ours and you have given us what is yours. Life and death, and death is life..."

It reminded me of childhood and the world my brothers inhabited. The scourge of bible talk.

"May these holy mysteries be pardon for your faults and cure for your death," the man said, Washington repeating his every word loudly, the voices seeming to bounce off the surrounding painted metal into the silence of the Georgia night sky above. "May you be strong for your voyage, son. May you be father to new souls..."

How to shift the direction of one's life, make the real changes you've spent years, decades even, promising everyone you're about to make. How can one shift the dynamics of one's story? Get beyond the cute lines and little melodies to not only create a fully structured song, but a whole album of original material. How to create a symphony, man, or a novel that people can look at and say, "Yeah, that's how it is. Things happen like that."

Even before being forced into this detour, I'd decided I'd had enough of the back roads. I was ready for I-95, the spinal cord of the east coast. I wanted a quick fix home.

I was on my knees being prayed over. Being offered my own tin foil cap.

"At least take the man's offer of an orange," said Jerry Washington. He'd explained to me, on the way here, how he spent time in a monastery before joining the clergy and getting excommunicated. Loved all the ritual, finding it like rock and roll's trappings.

I took the orange. Jerry led me away as the skinny reverend seemed to start speaking in tongues. By the time we exited a tin-foil shrouded gate complete with painted doll babies, shredded American flags and pulled-out cassette and unwound reel-to-reel tape fluttering in the breeze, the man was off in some singsong incantation, arms moving back and forth like some holy bowler.

"I know you need to be going, friend," Washington said, taking hold of my hands. "One dead man to another: stay clear. Climb that mountain."

And next thing I knew I'm back in the car, driving on the interstate watching the mile markers fly by. I wanted to stop my mind from getting pulled by these ancient memories of women, these fears for my kid and, worse, my worries about a fatherhood I should have dealt with earlier. I twiddled the radio dial, searching out a right-as-rain medley that would make for a perfect ride.

Pet Sounds. Perfect for bringing out the fan in me and some memories of the Wilson clan from back when we were all kings.

Dawn told me, just the day before, how much she liked it when I talked of the past. She said she loved hearing stories from the earlier days of rock and roll, when she wasn't yet old enough to be anything but a teen groupie. Liked it when I reminded her of the sullen jokester she'd seen hunkering down in home movies people had collected of the later tours. Or looking out, moon-eyed, on album covers. She loved me as a star, even if I was now falling. Or fallen. Her downed angel, her broken arrow, she cooed at me.

I tap my brake toe to *Wouldn't It Be Nice*, catching the glare from my red lights in the rear as I sail back home.

I'd started in with music when nine, a doe-eyed boy on a tree-shaded side street taking piano lessons on the family upright. Had my rise playing in a group at the ripe old age of 12 and never really stopped since. Made my first big money at 16. Wrote my best songs when I was 24, 25. I became star of the party. A party star. And then, all by my fucking self, an entire goddamned party.

The radio switches to *Act Naturally* by The Beatles. Yeah, they put me in the movies, too.

Now my kid's in those same years. Could he have fallen? Gotten hurt in some car? Seen his mother, my ex, with some new man that made him realize how much he wanted me? Or simply owed me, as his rightful father, as the man whose image and voice he'd have to carry through life?

I reach around and roll the windows down as I barrel up 95, part of the flow of trucks and night owls headed north. Air's getting chillier outside but no matter. I don't feel anything, really, except a nagging element of fear. The way the wind washes these thoughts loose.

Yes, Jerry Washington was the name of one of the guys I remembered reading an obit for. But maybe got the name wrong. Or didn't hear this new dude's name right, even if he looked right. Racism in action?

I feel the button indentations in the seat below my butt, behind my back. I watch the glow of the dashboard on my driving hand. Follow the red of the brake light as it reflects against my arm when I bop that pedal to the music. It's been a long, strange day and I wish I had company in the car with me once more, even if that company were but a ghost. Hell, I'd even play the ghost to a live companion. I don't want to get pulled into the past no more.

I remember driving places with Pa as a kid, what it was like to sit by him in the front seat as he talked. The smell and feel of him beside me. He never talked much but you could tell he wanted to tell me about Ma. Or about his own Pa.

I wish I'd driven with Junior. Maybe that's what this trip is all about...a second chance.

I flip off memory radio and buzz through stations for something new. *Night Shift* catches my attention. I sing along about Marvin Gaye. The song's about death.

I think about those of us caught in this boy-in-the-bubble-like thing. You want something to help the creative juices? You got it...up the nose, in the arm, down the gullet, withering off in a plume of smoke. Pay it later. It was all a company town. No one warned you that living's different from a record. Especially in a famous little town like Woodstock.

No one told me that there's a life after fame. That, like, rock and roll *can* die. That the arc goes both ways, and some people get as famous on the downswing as the up.

"You can be a loveable man when you let yourself," I heard Dawn saying as I rose from bed and headed into the shower. "I heard you sing it before I knew you. What happened?"

I should have sung her the song I was singing along to now, seven hundred miles north of that motel room in hot pursuit of something I wasn't quite sure of yet. I should have written the song myself.

I scribble what I can of its words: Gonna be OK. Not alone. It's the night. Everything shifts.

Oh, Dawn.

I've always gotten stuck in my head, even though my life's been an attempt to please my body. People loved the way I straddled anguish and swagger, pining hurt up against an artist's control.

All I could feel was me.

I was the skinny guy singing in high falsetto with eyes shut. Or looking away as my voice growled. Another guy on stage giving voice to scary things we all keep bottled. The everyman. A bottling juicer. Once I heard there were some who nicknamed me The Gobbler.

Who'd have guessed it would attract the sad sack fans of the hippie movement. I had just wanted the ladies.

Damn, Liz was traveling with me months after I asked if I could call her my girlfriend. She rode south with us in the station wagon, the two of us in the way back facing all we were leaving behind. She loved everything we came upon, even the flea-bit motel rooms where we'd be shacked up in one bed as Robbie, Rick, or Lee shacked up with their own model girlfriends in the other beds. We passed right through Civil Rights times. Would have been trouble if Levon weren't a southerner himself, ready to spout off and stand anyone down at a moment's notice. As could Ronnie, that gentle giant of a man who'd hired me and my brothers out of the small time up in Canada.

I wonder how my life would have been different were I born black, and not just Canadian.

Lizzie stayed on as best she could. But she wasn't ready to give up her life for mine. Just as I wasn't ready to accept responsibility for the consequences of my fun. Everything started happening all at once and the way things happen when you're young. We drifted on. And then apart.

Visible exhaust emanates from the cars I pass. Must be getting colder, although I don't notice my own breath.

I catch a long set of Dylan. The man I should have been. Could have been. Mystical and ever-changing, everlastingly productive. The unexpected survivor among us.

Visions of Johanna keeps me going as I sip a Stuckey's pecan shake topped off with three airplane bottles of bourbon. Sustenance. I was supposed to have been in the mix. He up and stole my best pointy suede fence-climbers. While on tour, no less. Round about the North Carolina border my central nervous system speeds up and I figure it's time for a rest stop. I need a long, rejuvenating, life-affirming bit of deep sleep. I aim for Pedro's South of the Border, a long time fave for us roadsters.

I don't make it to the motel. Just park the car by the giant restaurant's dumpsters and push the seat back. Knock off. Have a great dream, too, of these five naked, bald-headed women singing, with gauzy shrouds over their legs, on some long, flat black sand beach. I start to recognize what they're singing and sing along with it in spots as though it were something I was used to singing. But I'm hearing nothing. Just surf. The shrouded ladies' mouths open like baby birds in a nest, tongues wiggling like they were dying of some horrible plague or something.

I see the street I grew up on. First in snow, then in a hushed, summer haze. My Ma calls me. I'm singing that same song the naked women on the beach had been singing. Only the sound I hear this time is the sound of wind like breath over a wide-lipped bottle.

In. Out. In. Out.

I'm in a big field with Junior in my arms, a naked baby. There's a mountain in front of me. I know I'm supposed to climb it, but I don't know if I can with this kid in my arms.

There's a plume of smoke spiraling about in the sky and helmeted giants dancing out of it in some sort of victory shuffle. I feel like something's slipped inside of me.

I awake and get this flash of some big old car, like the ones I was crashing regularly during my brief battle with fame, Upstate. It's crumbling in slow motion, like one of those crash test dummy vehicles seen in driver's ed movies. I think I see a guy like me inside.

8

There's nothing like driving around old mountains on back roads in the wee hours before dawn, Klokko thought, naked as the day he was born. Especially when one's rain-washed and redolent with the magic scent of wild thyme.

He remembered bare-assed hippies from the Woodstock album cover, images of knights wearing armor seated by a forest pool, pages from his mother's moldy *Book of Knowledge*.

Klokko was on top of the world; clean and inspired. Wise, even. A model of God-blessed humanity, his beloved and loving cat on the front seat beside him. Like the subject of a song, one of those riffs you have to keep starting over to get it all. But you never can. It's just too perfectly matched to the emotions that led one to play it in the first place.

This wasn't a rare occurrence. Klokko had first driven naked a few nights after his Ma died, and again after his dad left. It came about the way it did this night. A cold rain. The ritualistic washing of himself in it. Sometimes there'd be mud. He didn't take the cat with him until recently because Beatrice had been afraid of him. Still more Gerard's kitty than his own companion and keepsake.

All changed, with time. Or so he thought this evening driving naked, wrestling with grander and even newer shifts in his life.

Klokko remembered his mission. He stopped the soundtrack to hear the simpler sounds of tires on gravel, and then asphalt; the swoosh of wet highways and then the sound of rain mixed with a sporadic clatter of ice on the car roof, on the windshield before him when he then decided to stop at the top of Durham Hill where the old Susquehanna Turnpike rolled out of the mountains into the wide valley of the Hudson, the distant streetlights of far-afield towns and Berkshire cities splayed out like fireflies before him.

Rural places die before the dawn. They're almost inanimate, except for the night creatures that crawl or slither for food. Owls that watch and swoop. Deer munching on gardens. Or he, Klokko, searching for ways to find love and roots. Memories. Dreams.

No one wakes for early chores until four. That's when farms start milking, wood deliveries begin moving around, dumping cords in people's driveways, laughing at the "You've got to be kidding!" reactions of city folks who still think morning starts after eight.

Klokko doubled back through North Settlement and climbed Clump Mountain, rolled down through Bone and Ghosty Hollows. Crossed county lines at a silent clip, deciding he'd had enough of silence. He was almost ready for what needed doing.

More music! Klokko reached into his box of 8-tracks, feeling for perfection. He put in a battered old relic without cover or name, a chicken-scrawl of handwritten notes on duct tape around one end. Joni Mitchell's *Hejira* and its mournful songs about black crows and Amelia Earhart, droned out against a meditative, elasticized symphony of jazzy intimations.

Beatrice stretched herself, then snuggled against her naked man's hairy leg. She purred with the music.

Usually, when Klokko came to the Old McDonald's farm crossroads, he sped straight through. Or made a right for a long meander back to Calvary. This time, Klokko slammed his brakes. In the road before him was a white owl looking straight into his headlights, unmoving.

The cat sounded in the seat beside him as her master instinctively reached across to keep her from slamming into the dashboard.

"Beatrice, my darling," Klokko whispered. He lifted the feline by the scruff of its fur. The cat looked at the owl and gakked.

Klokko noticed that one of the bird's wings seemed strangely folded. Its coloring, dirty white with specks of gray and black, matched that of the yard-high plowing detritus that surrounded the muddy crossroads.

"Ma said to watch for night owls," he said to Beatrice, opening the car door. Slowly standing, he carefully inched forward into the crossroads, naked. The owl followed his every move with what looked like imploring eyes.

Klokko stepped into the headlights' halo and stopped directly in front of the still bird. As he reached toward it a second owl swooshed in over the hood of the car, narrowly missing Klokko's head. The first owl rose, flapping its wings furiously, and flew up and over Klokko and his car. Beatrice made her strange, aged noise.

In the distance ahead, a worn down and tree-fuzzed mountain lit up from approaching car lights. The roiling noise of distant truck traffic sounded off in the direction of the interstate, ten miles distant.

The two birds fluttered above Klokko, then headed left down Old MacDonald's Road toward the highway. Toward Sid's Ford. Toward the object of his desires, the fount of all his dreams.

How to describe the way life pulls us? We're in our bed one moment, thinking about what could be, judging life by the song lyrics that seemed to lend everything a modicum of meaning, a wee bit of sense. And then we're naked in the middle of a dirt road, a battered Oldsmobile purring behind us.

Thaws raise hopes only to dash them. The chill always returns. Klokko's world.

The way he thought his actions out, everything develops, then unfolds. Fate was a game you couldn't win.

What happens happens, and then you get to work making some...any...sense out of the mess.

Klokko resumed driving as quickly as he could before a regular-world car came upon him.

He turned on his lights. Put in and sang along to his music, feeling as though his heart would burst from too much emotion, from way too many long years pent up.

When Klokko returned to his haunt by Sid's Ford, he parked and fixed his eyes on the dark window where his lady slept as though he could summon the sleeping young woman awake and across the road to him. As he dreamed about. He, naked. She...accepting and welcoming him thus.

Klokko blushed in the darkness.

Better, he felt, just to be here without explanation. For just another moment. It was that hour when no one stirred. His time. He was making changes, all right. He just wasn't fully sure if he was quite in control of them yet.

He took a whiff of the thyme emanating from his skin.

A passing milk tanker startled him. It was light already.

Across the roadway, a door opened on his lady's porch. A middle-aged woman stepped out backwards, yelling something inside.

"And you make sure you don't forget about returning all you borrowed," she yelled.

A man came out, groggy-eyed, tucking in his blue work shirt. He squeezed by the woman, threw his arms out and yawned.

Klokko recognized Gordon Mason, the guy who'd first stolen his given name of Richie and named him, who'd taunted him for his blushing and crushes. The guy who'd sentenced him to who he now was.

And then Klokko remembered that he wasn't wearing any clothes, and sitting with a cat in his old, parked Olds, at Sid's Ford. No dream, this. No romance.

He started sinking into the seat, wishing himself invisible.

Klokko's love walked through the door and onto the porch. She brushed her hair, talking.

The screams in Klokko's mind kept whatever words she was saying from his ears.

His girl with the reddish blonde hair stopped short of the stairs, her mother behind her. Gordon Mason stood to one side and scratched his balls.

She, his adored, was wearing a short skirt and a Cabbage Patch Dolls tank top. The mother said something about her not going to school dressed like some city tramp.

"Your father would never have allowed such a thing..."

Gordon stepped back and eyed the girl, warily.

"Looks okay to me, hon. Looks her age, y'know..."

Klokko's neck extended from his scrawny shoulders, his Adam's apple wobbling like a turkey's craw.

The girl stopped, looked straight across the road at his car. At him.

Klokko's head twisted full around and snapped back. Beatrice looked up at him and gakked.

Before he knew what he was doing, Klokko straightened up and keyed the car into action, peeling out and down the highway.

"Sheesh. I didn't even know there was anyone in that old car," said the girl, yawning and tugging at her skirt.

By then, Klokko, the cat, and the Delta 88 were a mile down the road doing ninety. He could just imagine what she said, over and over again in his head as fast as the yellow and white lines passed beside him heading home.

The sun rose quickly that morning, like it had to.

Some things don't change, he told himself. Like the seasons, like the sun.

The cat gakked.

"Like being buck naked in my car in broad daylight," he said, near tears. "Stupid, stupid, stupid me."

Klokko sped on.

9

There's a knocking at my window. I peer through glare-drenched glass at a young-faced, crew-cut guy in a leisure suit, smiling at me as though I was the second coming.

The sky's bright and cloudless. Behind the crisp young man are dumpsters spilling over with produce and cardboard boxes. Giant signs teeter up above announcing this location to those passing by at 70 along I-95. The car smells sickly, decaying. The seat is sticky from spilled milkshake, sour bourbon.

"It's never too late to repent, friend," crew-cut guy's saying. I wipe sweat off my brow, shake my head, and pull the seat forward.

"Look, I just wanted to check whether you were dead or not," the guy continues as I crank down the window. The morning chill wakes me further. "I'm half-joking about the repenting spiel. You need a cup of coffee or anything?"

"Just give me a sec and I'll meet you in the coffee shop," I say, nodding toward a circular, sombrero-shaped building.

I rub my eyes as he crosses the lot and disappears into glare. I adjust the mirror and check myself. Still older than I should be. Worse than I remember, in fact.

I run fingers through my hair, get out of the car. I bend a few times one way, then the other.

When I enter the coffee shop, guitar-heavy Mexican Hat Dance muzak bouncing lightly around the wide room, it takes me a moment to spot who I'm looking for. He's in a booth already, waving in my direction.

Dude starts talking as I approach, all about how he always stops at South of the Border every trip he takes up and down I-95—and that's a lot, given his line of work. He's always looking for someone to talk to and looking for ways he could do a good deed to make up for all his past mistakes. Didn't we all have enough of them already?

"You look bad, you know. Like you're in need of some good news," he says as I settle into the booth and open my menu. "Name's Bud. Bud Seaman."

I nod as he offers a hand.

"And you?" he asks. "Name, I mean?"

I tell him he can call me Al, if he really wants a name. He laughs.

"That's a good one. Could almost be a song..."

"Look, I'm sorry I'm not more forthcoming," I interrupt, glancing down to see what breakfast offerings are available. "I've got a lot on my mind right now. Bit groggy, still."

"Never you mind, Al. Just never you mind," Bud says, not skipping a beat and saying my name as if in 'quotes.' "We all have layers to work down through to get to what matters most. Me, I'm up and down this coast selling pineapple, jobwise, when what's really on my mind, and in my heart, is the spreading of Good News."

The waitress pours coffee as I brace myself for what I've spent a lifetime avoiding, and just escaped a few hours ago. The "good news" of the gospel. My salvation, God damn it. But I let him have his say. Why should I rain on his parade?

"I know what you're thinking, Al. I really do," Bud continues, pouring several creamers and saccharines into his already weak coffee as I sip mine black. "Here comes the Gospel again. Another attempt to bring the Good News of the Lord to you when you're most vulnerable and least able to fight it off. But that's not my purpose, friend. You looked like you needed some direction and had some questions that needed answering."

I take a long sip from my coffee then clear my voice as he holds my gaze.

"I, uh," I start, then clear my throat again. "I do. I do have questions."

"Don't we all, Al," Bud says, placing his hands on either side of his plate. "Where are you headed to?"

"Things have been strange, man, ever since I woke up yesterday. Got this strange summons, like, from an old man who said he'd gotten a call from my kid. I'm trying to get to him. Woodstock...that's where he lives. Me, too, when I'm not on the road."

I look down at my plate, avoiding Bud's intense gaze.

"I'm a musician," I say. "I've got this band, see. I made it kinda big once but now, we just play where we can. Things haven't been going all that well for some while now."

"It doesn't matter one bit, fame or no fame, Al, good times or bad," Bud says. The waitress approaches our table. "Your kid, is it a boy? You still with his mother?"

Bud excuses himself and orders a hamburger and potato salad. It still feels like morning to me, so I ask for huevos rancheros, extra hot sauce on the side.

"Don't worry about the bill," he says. "Expense account'll cover it."

"I've not been a good father, Bud," I say when the waitress leaves. "I've played my life too loose. I feel it's all slipped away from me, and I have nothing to show for shit. Sorry...for anything, I guess I mean. It's like I've never been able to live up to my creations, be it Junior, my kid, or any manner of songs I was once able to write. Used to be I took pride in what I was, in who people saw me as. Had a way of getting into the soul of whatever I did, stretching whatever was before me to draw out the spirit in it. But then it just got to where I'd be stretching whatever it was I faced just for the sake of stretching it, whether the thing should have been stretched or not. You know what I'm saying, Bud?"

Even though Bud didn't look like he knew, he nodded and told me to go on.

"It's all about clearing obstacles, Al," he said, stock-still before the window looking out on Pedro's busy parking lot, I-95 glinting with traffic in the distance. "I can tell you need to be clear. Go on."

"I guess I'm just feeling I failed my kid is all," I say. "I need a second chance, if such a thing is possible. Just like me and the boys have gotten with this tour, but on a personal level. Without any of the fame and pressure. Just to be a simple man, a good father is all."

"You can do it, Al," Bud says, looking away as the waitress approaches with our food.

The time's passed quicker than I think, as though my words have stretched out or I've said more than I can recall, or sense. He bites into his burger as I push my eggs around on the plate in front of me.

"I just want to write my own story, Bud, and stop getting pulled every which way by whatever seems to be happening, having no effect on what's going on around me," I say as Bud digs in. I glance down at the eggs before me. My appetite's dead.

"Even when it looks like we have no choices, we do," Bud says, mouth full. "Sounds like you're on a real journey, my friend."

"You buy fireworks?" is all I can reply, after a pause. I'm thinking of how I'd always wished my Pa had brought me fireworks, instead of just lecturing. "I'm feeling ready to buy some fireworks. For my kid."

So now I have this trunk full of fireworks, another go-cup in my lap. I'm back on 95, listening to what seems like an endless flow of Allman Brothers. I'm doing something with my life. I've bought Junior something he can't help but find somewhat cool. I hope.

That guy Bud, I've got to say, wasn't as bad company as I'd thought he might be. Made me laugh, the way he played along with that "Al" joke. But he also got me thinking with all his talk about just moving on, without worry about circumstances. Only then, he said, can you control what's happening.

I'd made a mess of things trying not to make a mess of things.

It turned out the guy's good news was less biblical and more wrapped up in this computer crap I've been trying not to pay attention to. He started telling me about the wonders of an age when photos will be "digitally captured" and transmitted over phone lines, like telexes and such. When records and tapes will be obsolete and folks won't be needing to record in studios anymore, not even with bands.

"Like synthesizers?" I asked. But Bud said "No, much more than that. You know what analog is?" And had I heard of this new thing called Intel and a company called Microsoft based out in Seattle and destined to push these newfangled, heavy-as-sin IBM personal computers and block-like Apple Macintoshes off into landfills.

No, was all I could reply. But I had heard they were able to determine paternity tests using those weird-looking things called DNA. And that cholesterol might not be as bad as everyone had thought.

It's getting dark again. A slight early March drizzle that would be snow were I home again, back where I'm headed, starts smacking up against the windshield. It's like the fog has followed me, seeped out from behind my eyes.

I even reached a point where I asked Bud Seaman about God and death and resurrection and original sin and forgiveness and fathers and sons and holy mothers. He begged off direct answers saying it all came down to faith, which he defined as "an undeniable belief in that which is most certainly true." Which felt like a duck.

Man, Gregg Allman's got a great soul growl, even if I get sick of all those doodling guitars after a song or two. Same with The Dead. Loved partying with those guys, sharing stages with them in those mega-concerts, that crazy train ride across Canada with Janis too drunk to even blow anyone.

I fish for hits. My taste's never really changed, I guess. I'm a sucker for the sentimental, be it Johnny Ray or Ray Charles, Bobby Bland or Teddy Pendergrass. I like to croon.

White soul's the thing these days. Keyboards and drum machines. I could be a contender again.

I wonder what my boy's up to now, at this very moment. Watching TV after school? Eating Lizzie's brownies laid out on the

Moroccan rug I'd gotten her a few weeks before that last straw? Playing with some puppy that's been trained not to shit all over the lawn, let alone in any Woodstock superstar's shoes, like the one my bandmates gave me once.

I'd like to think my life was a mystery and me this charming, fedora-wearing detective sort trying to figure it all out. The way those German directors paint us Americans. Or the way everyone likes to lead their lives, now that we've been through a century of increasingly complicated plotlines, all seemingly derived from life but, in reality, just the devices of money-hungry artists with too many mouths to feed. "Artists" making their living, throwing shit together to feed bad habits picked up on the way up or down.

Like the songs I should have been writing. Could have written, were it not that something gave out inside of me oh so many years ago.

"I feel your body move. I say what I always say," I scribble, stealing from the radio. "Don't go away. Don't take this part of me..."

It's night, and a mess of top-forty songs later, by the time I start heading around the D.C. Beltway. I try listening to the local politi-talk but get lost in the names. Bob Dole, Robert Byrd, Alan Simpson, Alan Cranston, Tip O'Neill, Jim Wright, Tom Foley, Trent Lott. Snores.

There's not too much one can do pro-actively with your life when driving on an interstate, except maybe straighten some of it out. And not get killed.

I get to thinking about how it was on the road back when I could score so easy it made my head spin. Liz must have known. But it wasn't such that did her wrong. She didn't really start to get worried until Mickey Twist came along with his fine-tooled shoulder bags. Over at Levon's, after things kicked off with the record contract in '67, when everyone got to talking about what stars we'd be. The future I was bound to have.

Later, the two of us nestled in bed before heading out to Malibu, around the time we must have conceived Junior. I started channeling this strange country dude I'd conjured out of the places and people we'd passed by up in the mountains outside Woodstock. My biggest fan, this dude. Shaped his whole life around everything I sang. Pieced him together from a sad-sack kid I remembered from school and what I imagined my dad saw when he'd look at me. Made him shy and strange and scarecrow-like, not fully in control of his body. Played off my own physique, giving him this extra-long neck and bulging eyes. Skinny, like I've always been.

We laughed long and hard about that. And then actually made love, instead of simply fucking, as it often was when it was she and me and the drink.

I think the guy was my other me, part the oaf who kept Mickey Twist's number in his head, part the fuck-up who had to stay quiet every few gigs or so, given my inebriation on stage. My fright-self, I called him.

Sure, this dude also came up out of the crazy times that swirled a-plenty before Lizzie settled my life. Spun-out cars on back roads. Naked drives through town at mid-day, everyone looking but not looking.

How many times DID I hide fully clothed in the shower when Officer Bill came by?

Two girls at once? Three? A lit foot trying to barbecue for the boys?

I pass a shining Oz-like monstrosity, gold-lit and windowless behind a scrim of pines. The Mormon Tabernacle. I've always felt somehow blessed when I pass that thing.

You get to where you're doing shit just to test yourself, to see if you're still alive. Same thing as when the conversation's gone all quiet after sex, or in the morning before you're out the door, and the best you can do to get things hopping is pick a fight. Answering every statement with a question and such.

Strange how I'm now hoping such shenanigans stop with me and don't pass through my kid. Ain't it always so?

I need to get on with this journey. I turn the music off as the lights of the long Baltimore tunnel draw me on.

I think back to another barbecue, in an old barn Mickey Twist had moved into. Everything fine at the time. Money flowing so fast and steady I was sure we'd all be retired by the time I hit 30. Taken to driving a Ferrari. Everything seemed like it had all come together. A stretch of verdant lawn. Big old pines and hemlocks whispering in a slight breeze. Blue sky going dark, its clouds taking on an increasingly reddish hue. Kids playing everywhere. Talent all around. Everybody famous, in their own ways.

I was talking, drink in hand, on and on about the beauty of life. It was there for anyone. You just had to smooth the rails to sail down to it. And then Mickey stepped off the porch among us and we all let *him* talk, and laughed at everything *he* said, because we knew that no matter how many songs we wrote or sang, how many records we sold or concerts we played, he was the one with the power. He had what we all needed, you see, somewhere inside that giant, expensively rethought barn. The only reason we were all here, really, laughing at *his* jokes and letting our kids play in *his* yard, were *his* drugs. The *real* power.

And as soon as I understood that it was like I suddenly noticed my wife looking into me. And Liz did this thing with her eyes that told me it was time to change. But I just knew I couldn't. Because, like, my feet were cemented there. I still had a drink to finish. The talk was good and the sky beautiful. I wanted to sail in my Ferrari.

I've got a lot to reckon with. And for. This isn't going to be easy, I figure.

I'm now into that stretch of Maryland where Our Lady of the Highways shines over passing sinners. One of my eyes is open for it. The other's searching deeper inside, like that balloon eyeball I saw a painting of once. Or that thing topping the dollar bill's pyramid.

I can get the Philly stations. Good timing because I need to lose this train of thought and settle on a power play of Sade. She gets me, that smooth-as-silk operator

And what do you know, my mind's onto how strange it was the way we met, Dawn and I, on the Sunset Strip not far from Sammy Davis Jr.'s house in the Hollywood Hills where Liz and I used to go for our afternoon walks that winter we all talked our manager and record company into letting us record in luxury. In Hollywood, no less. What were we thinking? Fame was us. Our ambition had no boundaries. I liked the buzz of it all, the better wines and drugs. The ogling eyes of starlets, even if I was content to stick with my model wife...pretty much.

Dawn had come up in that crowd, but on its lower, harder side. Liz and I and the boys were spending time with Steve Stills and David Crosby, Peter Tork, the Wilson brothers. L.A. was fast and fun, not wrapped up in the politics or strange in-crowd wariness of the Bay area, even though that's where the best gigs were.

Dawn was one of those high school cuties you'd see outside the Whiskey. The sort that didn't care whether you were a lead singer or a drummer, a dance choreographer on the Bob Hope show or some extra from *Bonanza*. It's a good thing Dawn never met Charlie Manson. Or learned how to make plaster casts.

We got together, figured we'd been fucking in the same motels for years. You could see it in how she'd aged so damn well, filled out with a sensuousness I was finally ready for—after carrying Liz all over our form of Hades long enough to nearly break my back, if not my spirit.

She could have been my savior, my muse out of the mess I had made of my dreams.

Or Lizzie reduxed.

I decide to short cut up the Delaware River to Port Jervis. It's getting towards dawn again, that first sense of light starting to seep across the sky, and I'm hankering for eggs and bacon. My meal, breakfast. Any drunk's meal, if you ask one.

I'm finally beyond the blackouts far enough to feel comfortable with myself again. Or whatever that was in the bathroom yesterday.

I jolt when a siren sounds and police lights start a-whirling. I check the speedometer as it moves down from 60 in what must have been a 45 zone. I pull over into a parking lot for Washington's Crossing State Park. Turn the radio down. Put the go-cup under the seat in that stealthy way that shows no movement from the waist up. Roll the window down by the time the sheriff's deputy is standing by my rent-a-car door, a flashlight shining in my face.

"How the heck are you this fine morning, officer," I blurt out in a yokel half-laugh, another mannerism learned from years of such pull-overs.

"Well, where do I start," says the baby-faced but middle-aged policeman, his hat jauntily cocked on his bullet head, his body trim in its uniform. "This here a rented car?"

"Driving up from Florida, headed to Woodstock, New York," I answer. "Just a shade passing through."

"Short-cutting from the Turnpike, I take it," the cop says, warming up faster than I'd expected. "Woodstock, eh? Why, my favorite bands are from up there."

I hum a few bars of *Lay Lady Lay* and the deputy steps back, a big grin breaking across his face.

"You don't say," he says. "Why, I should have known you the moment I laid eyes on you."

"It's been some time, you know," I answer, realizing it HAD been over a decade since my last new recording hit the record bins, not to mention the fact that I'd never sung that song. Could he really think I was Bob Dylan? Or did it matter?

"You know, I got a little something you might want if you're feeling tired there, friend," he adds, easing his posture and taking on a winking demeanor. "Picked it off some kids up the river in Lambertville earlier this evening."

I smile wide, wishing I could take him up on his offer but knowing better. Besides, I'm just not that tired. Too much of the stuff coursing through my veins already, I guess. It's like I've been pickled in formaldehyde, as far as my bod goes.

"No thanks, Officer, I quit," I reply. "You wouldn't happen to know a good spot for breakfast that would be open round about now?"

He tells me to keep heading north until I hit 202, then east ten miles into Flemington. It was all that would be open, he says apologetically, until at least seven. I thank him and, thinking quick, ask if I could sign a ticket for him.

"Oh, I won't be writing none, seeing it's you," the cop says.

"But Officer Matthews," I reply, with a wink. I learned years back to read those name tags but fast. "I'm thinking a little autograph could get you places yourself."

He blushes and hands me a blank ticket, which I sign and hand back. I start feeling the chill of the March air as the adrenaline seeps out of me. There's still splotches of old snow laying around under trees here. I'm getting back into the world of seasons now...almost.

"You know, if you're looking for a bit of fleshy comfort," he says. I flash him a smile and shake my head.

"Got a ways to go, yet," I tell him, not wanting to push my luck any further. I've still got hours to drive before I get home. Don't want to thin myself out any more.

"You know, I think I just read something about you today. Maybe heard it on the radio," the cop says. I nod and start pulling out.

"Yeah, the radio..." I hear him saying as he vanishes from view in my mirror. "Said you had..."

I don't catch the rest. I've got the radio back on. *Billy Jean*. But for some reason, I turn off the highway as soon as I'm out of his sight, sensing something wrong. I pull behind a warehouse and cut the engine and lights as his squad car zooms by, siren and flashers on.

I double back the way I came and cross into Pennsylvania just south of where our first president, years ago, did the same. I think about heading out to Valley Forge, which I remember from Junior's school books. But then another chill hits my spine.

Time's running out.

I've got to see my boy. I've got so much, now, to tell him.

10

Klokko saw little but his car's movement on asphalt, gravel, and white, sandy dirt as he drove that first hour out of Sid's Ford. His heart raced, his tires, bouncing and spinning faster than his thoughts, as he peeled farther and farther away, sure there'd be a posse of angry, unshaven men and screaming women with pitchforks after him, carrying a big rail to ride him on once they got him gummed up with tar and sprinkled like a chicken with several pillows' worth of feathers.

Beatrice stood on her hind legs, front paws on the dashboard, caterwauling like some banshee.

Klokko knew, the moment he peeled away from his beloved reddish-blonde lady in the early morning glare, that there was no way he could go home. Gordon Mason would figure where he'd be. No home for now, he reasoned.

When you want change, change happens. The trick is to figure out just how one might control it.

Klokko hit the back roads he knew and took them out to where his knowledge and memory faded. He followed the map he'd been building in his head all 42 years of his life. It was a map he'd been perfecting, lying in the dark in his red room at night; his great artwork, his long-planned-for but never executed outlaw act of driving cross country without plates. He'd planned it for his grandpa's old Studebaker, out in the barn, until the barn collapsed in on the classic car and the plan had shifted to an old station wagon his dad had picked up in Woodstock from some hippie types. They'd said the car had traveled all through the south, carrying some band from gig to gig. He never could get it started, though. Its transmission was shot.

Tracked from the heavens, Klokko's path would look straightforward and ultra-logical, always making the beeline between two spots, even if, on ground, the roads he took looked like country lanes, overgrown driveways, forgotten pathways from a distant past. Rural ways past.

The Delta 88 climbed over the narrow, hemlock-canopied back roads of the northwestern, central, and then southern Catskills. Up past places called Moon Haw and Watson Hollow, the potholed Peekamoose road into Sullivan County. Then down onto little used country lanes through what was once the Borscht Belt, now nothing but ghost towns surrounded by haunted hotel behemoths and a smattering of orthodox encampments of various sects and denominations, disguised as bungalow colonies.

As he drove, calmed by so many directional choices, Klokko started to wish that he'd picked up some real religion back when he was forced to attend churches and revivals, Sunday Schools and prayer meetings. He could have used a bit of faith and fervor to counter the obsessiveness with which he approached his loves with no counterweight to keep him from tumbling into the despair he now felt. He wished he'd never learned how good it felt to take himself into his own hand and roll over onto amassed pillows, shooting his load into an old towel thinking only of love.

Klokko wished he'd never drunk the whiskey that was his Pa's bane. Otherwise, he'd still think of his disappeared father, and himself, as good men. He wished he'd never taken a hit of the pot that Gerard had fallen so enamored of, leading him into all that other bad stuff that ended up killing him. And with his death, Ma's. How had he become a man filled with so many regrets?

He almost wished the weed and drink hadn't made the music so big in his life. Such a force of understanding. And misunderstanding. A soundtrack without any movie.

He wished he had nothing but his love. And had his love without even the girls he loved for the sake of Love.

Klokko wished he wasn't now driving naked in bright sunlight. With a cat by his side. With no spare change.

Driving into the open spaces of former dairy lands, away from the mountains he'd known his whole life, Klokko pushed his mind deeper into his story.

How had he come to this, wasting his life loving women only from afar? Had Gerard been a wanker, like he was? Or his father? Gordon Mason, maybe, but certainly not his Pa.

Klokko thought about his mother as he emerged onto a tree-canopied creekside roadway. Was there something *she* never got from his father, and vice versa? Why had Pa left at a point when he should have gotten a grip on his son's and wife's deaths? Another woman? Or had he simply imploded, the way Klokko now felt falling in on himself? Had he washed himself in the rain and driven off naked? Perhaps, he thought, change was simply like this...abrupt and unknowable. A leap of faith. A scared jump into someone else's narrative, trusting all will turn out well and the fates don't have any worse tragic turns to throw one's way.

Klokko shoved in an old Leonard Cohen 8-track he'd picked up in a box at some yard sale near Woodstock years back. The stuff soothed him. It matched the thaw that was drawing him south for reasons he had yet to question.

Klokko remembered each of the women he'd loved. Marianne, the red-haired one with pigtails, who sent him a Valentine in sixth grade. He loved her, silently, for four years until she told him she wished he was dead if he didn't stop.

"So Long, Marianne."

Then Melissa, with her soft ears poking through straight, black hair in ninth grade English class. He would try not to breathe when thinking of her so no one, let alone she, would ever know and hate him, too.

That song The Band did, about being on a mountain and tasting his love's hair, was all about Melissa. How could such a love ever be refuted, and never be allowed to blossom? As well as *"Sweet Melissa,"* who the Allmans sang to, and about, before they crashed and burned.

Klokko remembered loving the woman he worked with one summer cleaning toilet stalls at Camp Timberland. She had curly hair, a laugh like a waterfall. She lived in another state but came back three summers. He loved her year-round.

He loved her two times, as the Doors sang.

All the others...

By his reckoning, the river he was following now must be the Delaware. On the other side was Pennsylvania. A whole new state, another change. He'd have to cross quickly to avoid traffic, towns, and the prospect of someone spotting his nakedness. He spun east, remembering that, by the maps he knew, there was an old aqueduct crossing a few miles from where he'd emerged. A place with almost no traffic, especially on a morning like this. A place where only one car could pass over the river at a time.

Klokko realized he'd just driven a half hour without music. All he'd been hearing in his head was a giant screeching. In it, like a single cricket in a chorus of tree frogs, his beloved's voice, heard for the first time, was as lilting as a lullaby.

The Leonard Cohen tape had snapped in the machine. He threaded out the rumpled 8-track, rolled down his window and tossed it, watching in the rearview as the tape broke open and unfurled on the asphalt like a broken nest of snakes.

Klokko wanted to kill Gordon Mason for being in his love's house. Gordon Mason had always had the girls. They said he had bad-boy charisma. He knew how to hold a woman just right. Dumb shit, he thought. Klokko knew that Gordon Mason knew nothing of love. Just lust.

Had his father been a man like that, he wondered? As Klokko moved along the highway looking for his crossing, he pondered his parents. "No," he said aloud, his first spoken words in hours. "They were good people. Trapped people."

Beatrice gakked her approval.

Enough of others' music. He needed to straighten out the sound in his own head for a change, Klokko figured.

He saw the Roebling Aqueduct up ahead, an old stone struc-ture with wooden sides built by the master architect who would later design the Brooklyn Bridge. A car came down the hill on the opposite bank, readying to cross. Another stream of traffic headed his direction. He slowed, not wanting to draw attention. He stopped, opened the window a crack to let the chill air remind him of his danger, the oddness of his situation...naked in an old car, cat screeching by his side, headed into Pennsylvania at mid-day just before Spring's long-awaited arrival. A music freak with his tapes snapping.

The car emerged from the aqueduct and Klokko sped across and up the opposite side, vanishing as soon as possible onto more back roads.

He was riding fine, missing all dead ends. No thoughts, or regrets, involving the future or past.

He noticed the gas gauge. Nearing empty.

The cat gakked.

Her gauge was down, too. No mice in a Delta 88. No scraps to throw her way.

He was no glutton, Klokko. But everyone gets hungry, every once in a while. Everything's just got to get some fuel sometime to move forward.

Only when a fellow's well-tuned to one place can he start to notice the subtle changes that make life rich. Klokko stretched his thinking to ponder; landscape to landscape, setting to setting, person to person, story to story. He would traverse the back roads of Pennsylvania intent on finding food and fuel, thinking about what direction he might now be taking his life.

What might be pulling him? Had this all come from his own actions or was something else in play?

Klokko pondered the possibility of a greater being, a higher purpose to all he did, thought, and couldn't do.

He certainly knew that there was an element of fear, of his life's big mistakes and fate, that was pushing, or maybe pulling, him down the road at such a clip. That had always been so. Sometimes visible, other times not.

Klokko had been taught the chivalric code by his mother. It inspired action when he needed direction. He'd be Roland, or Gawain. His actions were to demonstrate valor, courage, and his undying passion for Love, whether the woman he loved knew of his feelings or not. He dreamed, always, of great actions which he would have to travel to find. Or grow to meet.

Countless were the times Klokko dazed away in class, dreaming that his school was under attack by Russians or spacemen, with only him to save the day and gain the admiration of Marianne, Melissa, or whoever else had his fancy. It's what kept him going through his brother's and mother's funerals. What kept him from retching as he cleaned the grotty camp toilets during those summers he loved the curly-haired girl from some weird-sounding place in Pennsylvania.

He would find her!

Dawn, he recalled. Her name was Dawn. She'd moved to someplace in Florida. I'm on a quest to Florida, he told himself. I'll find Pa!

Beatrice gakked in the seat next to Klokko, as if affirming his thoughts. Or puking them back up.

The fuel gauge was on E. Things were critical.

Klokko pulled to a stop by the Delaware, high trees all about him and a glimmer of rushing water in the distance. He lifted the cat as he gathered the blanket he'd been sitting on around himself. He wrapped himself in it, adjusting the mirror to check himself out. Weird, but better than he'd been.

There was a black car with Florida plates parked up ahead, no one in it. He pulled back onto the road, passed the empty car, and rifled through his glove compartment as he steered with one hand. Tapes. Pennies and dead fuses. His father's old pair of thick black sunglasses!

He put them on, feeling rock-star.

But then Klokko started weeping. Slowly, at first, but then with building emotion. Why, he caught himself thinking for the first time in a decade, had his daddy left? It was bad enough that Gerard died. And then his mother. But why did his dad go, and to where?

Klokko entered the outskirts of a small city. He felt himself getting pulled towards fast food joints and chain convenience stores. Full-service gas stations.

This, he thought, was the world his father drove away to and never returned from. Had he died, caught in some accident like Gerard, or just chosen to forget him, moving on beyond the pain of two deaths and a useless son?

Klokko had figured out how to get money. Checks came in from his mother's social security account and the disability account she had set up for him. Everyone said it had something to do with his knees, but he knew the tests were for smarts. Which he didn't have. Just the ability to love and to feel the power of rock and roll.

Klokko'd been through a drive-in fast-food place once before. Remembered that you ordered by talking at a sign and then picked up your food at a window. If he just timed it right, he could make a getaway and pay everyone back later. Simple. The gas would be another matter.

He had to keep moving so the tears wouldn't return, streaming down his grizzled cheeks beneath his father's shades.

Convenience stores gave way to strip malls and giant stores larger than he'd ever imagined. Ameses and Caldors and K-Marts, Super Ks. Big as deserted old resorts and factories, these places. And fast-food choices beyond his capability to choose. Wendy's and Burger King and Hardee's and McDonald's and Pizza Hut and Perkins. He pulled up to a Dairy Queen, having heard the name, but saw there was no drive-through window.

Klokko hit the highway again, worried about the increasing amounts of traffic starting to swirl about him. He U-turned at an intersection, having spotted a McDonald's. That's where he'd seen the drive-in windows he was thinking of.

Fortunately, there was only one car ahead of him when he pulled into the take-out line. He pulled up to an inner-lit menu board as a flat girlish voice welcomed him and asked what he would like that day.

Klokko went gruff and growly, his voice cracking as he spoke. "Hamburger. Three hamburgers. French fries, please. Two of 'em," he said.

"Large, medium, or small?" the voice from nowhere asked. "Three regular hamburgers or do it all with cheese?"

"Big," Klokko responded, his neck growing longer out of the blanket that wrapped his nakedness. The cat cowered below the seat. "Big fries. Big burgers."

"Would you like a drink with that?" the female voice returned.

"Milk," said Klokko. "Three milks."

"And can we get you anything else today?" asked the voice. "We've got a special on Chicken McNuggets in the 9-pack. Plus, we can Big Mac Special the rest of it all."

"Yeah. McNuggets. Big Mac Specials," Klokko said, starting to fall in love with the disembodied voice.

Beatrice gakked from below the seat.

"Two of the nugget things," Klokko added.

"That will be $11.68. Please pay at the first window. Thank you and have a nice day," added the feminine voice.

Klokko wondered what she would look like as he started to pull forward. He pulled up to a window where a smiling old man with thick glasses opened the glass and held out a mottled hand.

"$11.68, please," he said in a gruff voice.

Klokko's neck lengthened tight, then sprung. No, no, he thought. Not now. This is wrong.

He peeled away, around the next window where his food was surely waiting, and darted out into traffic.

The cat meowed hungrily.

After five or six turns, Klokko pulled behind a Shoprite and parked by the dumpsters.

"We'll get you something later, sweetness," he said to his cat.

He turned the Oldsmobile's engine off and tried to think clearly.

His Pa had talked of Philadelphia once. He'd shipped out of there during his War years. Got to know fellows who talked about how there was always work in those parts. He'd even met a girl, before he met Ma, who lived in a place of mansions called Bala Cynwyd. Took the train out, walked up this big hill through a crowded, brick-built town and down an old tree-lined street of giant houses. Took one look at the girl's and turned around to head back to base.

"But Pa, you said Ma was your first and only love," Klokko said to his father in those days after the woman's sad passing.

"That's true, boy," Pa replied. "But there are always paths you never feel right taking. Then never let go of."

"But what about now," the son asked, afraid how his father might answer.

"Maybe now," his father said, looking down. "Maybe now I'm ready."

Klokko turned the engine on. He had to do something. The traffic was heavy but moving steadily.

Finally, Klokko had a real plan brewing in his head.

11

The sun rises over the misty tree-covered roadway. The stone-studded Delaware River rushes on. I'm wrapped in softness about everything that's pulling me. Whatever it was with Junior couldn't be all bad or I'd have heard from his mother. Each time I phoned her, in South Carolina and in Maryland after getting more gas (again, they declined my card. What gives?), her voice sounded sad but not panicked, as I know she'd be if something had happened to our kid. It was just that tone she'd get whenever *I* was in trouble. As though *I* weren't actually talking and all she could hear was silence.

What could the boys be thinking back in Winter Park, two days after having to abruptly cancel a gig because of my unexplained absence? They'd been pushing for this tour, this reunion, because they felt it would be good for me. But also, fun. And here I am, gone AWOL after only a month.

Fortunately, we know each other well enough to realize it could have been any of us (except Garth, of course). We'd have kept right on with whoever WAS there, as we'd done many a time over the years. And had planned even before Robbie abandoned us.

We all end sometime. The Beatles broke up. The Rascals, the Lovin' Spoonful. Simon and Garfunkle and several versions of Mick Fleetwood and John McVie's band before they hit the jackpot hiring a California couple. No one lasts, with most groups splitting before marriages. Hell, next up to leave would probably be Rick who always seemed to enjoy walking the edge better than landing either side of it.

It's one of those late winter mornings when you feel Spring on its way. Blue skies beckon me north and out of this damned coffin of a car. Steam rises off what snow is left by the roadsides. Ice is breaking along the edges of the river, with only a few stray floes racing down the Yoo-hoo murk of the high water.

Not much on the radio. I scatter away from the news like birds from gunfire and land on another power ballad that seems right for the moment.

It's some Scandinavian band, from where a king just got shot if I remember right.

"Take me," I scribble, messing with the lyrics I'm singing along to. "Let me go."

What was with the cop? Jerry and Bud and the old dude Cato, now so far back in time that he's as ghostly, in my memory, as that Vincent Price character who seemed to occupy my backseat for a good third of Florida? This has been fucking weird. Could there be lessons here for me to learn? Was Officer Matthews trying to tell me it's my choice to go with the flow or not?

Bud seemed to say that no matter the choice, the important thing is action, or those computer thingies he kept going on about. Jerry Washington showed me that it was never the performance that was important, but the way that performance, or those songs I got down to write and record, captured an emotion others could share. That shit, he seemed to say, was a gift. The emotions. The sharing.

I can't get my mind out of the bad corners I've been avoiding for far too long. What do you tell your son when you've never really spoken with him? Is it too corny to say a simple "I love you, kid?" Ask questions? My Pa could never do it so why should I think I have that gene? It would be easier speaking from the grave, as I'd often wished my Pa could have done for me.

Once, I took flowers to his gravesite. Nice place but I wanted to get away from the spot almost as soon as I got there. He'd left room, I found out, for me and my brothers next to him and Ma.

The radio fuzzes out and I skirt Stroudsburg, start into the Water Gap. It's pretty much a ghost road now, all surrounding farms and villages emptied of people, razed. Started years back as a reservoir project, then some kind of national park. Not that different from the way I've grubbed my memories of Ontario. All razed.

I pull over to piss, stepping down an embankment over crusty blackened snow to where the ground feels spongy. I nestle in behind some barren oaks, a bit of ironweed still red from six months earlier. I hear the river but can't see it. No birds. My piss steams as it streams through the chill air. I try to write something with it in the snowbank but end up with nothing more than an elliptical trail that reminds me of that tragic Challenger plume run awry.

Had that moment made us all hackneyed skeptics?

I hear a vehicle and step behind an oak. Why tempt fate any more than one needs to? I spot a grim face rush past in a blur of dedicated, forward-motion travel. I stand a while and listen as the silence returns.

A rustle in the branches above and the distant whoosh of the river's rising.

It was magic, moving up to the country 20 years ago. Dredged up memories of dirt forts and hideouts, the fields out where relations still kept farms, to make me feel renewed. Got me hiking into the woods, riding a bike to and from town like when I was a boy. Collected acorns and acorn caps and moss and colored leaves; made box presents for Lizzie, even for Bob and the boys when we holed up in that pink house's basement under the Wall of Manitou.

I had this spot I'd go up to on the haunches of Overlook, where quarrymen had dug out the native bluestone and left a castle-like wonderland of slag heaps and birch trees, water dripping down etched walls muted by soggy moss. You could see off to the Hudson from there, glimpse the distant Taconic Hills. A church spire down in town. The distant thrum of traffic and an occasional jet stream mixing with clouds as though trying to become one. I took Lizzie there and wrote a song from the experience. Found a handful of other tunes with help from the wind, the rustling trees, the sense of loneliness I came to treasure, briefly. Help from Bob, too. Robbie...

Saw a snake slithering over the rocks one time, a bear clambering up the hillside another. I stopped climbing. Never liked the idea of either beast; I was enough of one to deal with. I turned my back on nature, except for the beach out front of the house we rented in Malibu, or the sides of roads such as this where I'd riff on the wild a moment, needing to piss.

I wondered if my kid played outdoors or stayed at home with the Mario Brothers, with Pong? Sure, we played catch some when he was younger, before he could know how lousy I was at any sport.

I'd take him to playgrounds. The movies down in Kingston once or twice.

I get back in the car and ride quiet up into New York State. Head up through little towns that feel oddly familiar. Keep by the river, then head up a branch past some weird stone bridge as the skies fill with clouds and a light rain starts to fall. I see a sign for Bethel, the biblically named site where we all descended in helicopters to play for a half million like us. Like *us?* Really?!?

What could I tell my kid about all that? What would I have read Junior if I'd been a reader, and not a singer? Or a real writer, like all the critics had said I could be? Not the party itself, as I explained myself to others.

I'd like to have made up Rumpelstiltskin. I loved the way he gave and took treasure. Sorrowful little man, all hairy scary until ruined by his own greed and lack of control. Could it have been Old Rumpie's offspring who became the dwarves in Rip Van Winkle, haunting these Catskills I used to love so.

I'd have also tried my hand at the Bible, those stories having stayed with me somehow, even if muted by my own adventures over time.

What was that cop who offered me coke trying to say when I left? Heard something about me after all these years? I mean, was I getting some sort of recognition for my work with The Place, that rehab center for drug problem kids Joe got me to do a benefit for? Even though I would have been happy to score whatever it was that had gotten them in there in the first place?

I want to get back into the day-to-day challenges of life, embrace the straight people, the drivers and pharmacists, waitresses and traffic cops, who have always answered my slurred questions with admonishing looks and questions and statements like "Is that so?" or "That's certainly commendable," while all the while I'd be seeing the Paxil and Tuinal, the Demerol and Valium surging behind their eyeballs, the liquor rising out of their breath and skin. Once addicted, the world reveals its addictions.

It's been a fucking nightmare trying to go straight. It's worked for stretches. I simply couldn't keep it up. Can't.

Why am I worrying about this yet again?

Junior. The terrain starts to roll, and mountains rise, bare branched, over the road, I'm a lost man.

I need YOU, kid.

I pass old hotel buildings shuttered and crumbling, bungalow colonies swallowed by sumac.

Junior had my Hawk-look from the moment I laid eyes on him, swimming out from Lizzie's inner self like some gloppy albino golliwog. And he had me down for the fool father I was always to be right from the start. When he got a bit older, stumbling about our rented houses, he'd move all arms a-flopping, as if imitating me, the big man of his life. He'd get a pained look on his face, shutting his eyes and screeching the way I saw myself, on film or in my head, singing. Eventually, he'd sing too, my kid.

Entering the deep Catskill forest after the fallow farms and ripped-apart Borscht Belt hotels of Sullivan County, I realize how much I've missed the Woodstock we had. Rick had brought me back but all the talk about old days was too much. Along with all the ghosts of partiers past. And the parties now gone.

We stretched royalty checks as best we could. Lived on credit, hoping for a comeback. Renewal. Eyes on that Rock and Roll Hall of Fame thing to make sure our time would come, like the $200 you pick up passing GO as a saving grace. Paraded around town like the stars people still considered us to be, and which we could still see in ourselves with proper lubrication.

I should never have grown old. I should never have stopped getting my way with the songwriting credits while I was ahead of the game. That was the drugs talking. Lee had always said we should have paid more attention to the business side of things. Same with Liz, even when I said Ricky was the man for that. "Rick?" she'd yell. "You mean that heap of a man crashed out in our driveway night after night?"

Our first comeback concerts, following a couple of gigs down at the Lone Star, had me all excited about practicing again, at least for the first weeks. It allowed me to lose my old fears of not being the writer everyone wanted me to remain. I played at just being a performer with an aging bluesman's way of interpreting chestnuts, pointing others in the direction of all the good things we'd uncovered. Ain't taste, after all, the big cheese of our day?

I got together with Carole and Gerry, didn't I, a sure-as-shit sign that the old juices were flowing again. Wrote a sweet song together. Too bad no one released it.

I'd had a good time playing in Saugerties before the boys pulled me back on the road.

But maybe I've gotten my latest break too late.

The mountains return. I enter a narrow valley. More swatches of cruddy snow along a larger highway barreling fast by some town called Roscoe. Maybe it's that roadway's anonymous rush that gives everything, once again, the nasty look the Northeast gets in late winter before the true promise of spring hits.

But still, the warmth rises.

Why in hell was I returning to this Purgatory?

I had to get things in order and climb that mountain, as old man Cato said. Deal with shit, for once. Didn't someone once tell me that anyone who slept in the shadow of Woodstock's mountain, that rising known as Overlook, was always destined to return? Was fated, moreover, to be buried within that same shadow?

Instead of trying to figure out how to get home from here, or hitting that fast four-lane, I head into town thinking there might be a HoJo. I'm dying for clam strips. Everything's dripping, snow melting in the bright-again March sun. I sluice down a main street towards something shiny—a big pool of water where two rivers converge, the highway's sweeping bridge lending the scene a certain quiescence. I pull up to a brick building labeled Antrim Inn.

Sometimes a man just needs a drink, a soul-to-soul with a trusted barkeep. Even if it's not quite midday yet.

There's a strange creature carved into the inn's sign: a fish with two heads, one looking one direction, the other impassively staring at the other. I park adjacent to the water and check myself, instinctively, in the rearview. I'm there, alright: a skull gleaming through a shroud, the specter of death caught shining beneath graying skin.

There's no one at the bar when I enter. I slap my arms warm as much out of habit as for any actual feeling of chill. For a moment, settling in at a stool and searching the dark edges of the lit area for a bartender, I'm ready to populate the place with my own memories.

"It's slow this time of year. Makes a man wish he were elsewhere," comes a nasally, high-pitched voice from the darkness. "Some say it's a sign of the economy, a call for development, if you catch my drift."

A face moves into the light, and I could swear it's Albert Grossman, the former manager we buried just a month ago. Same strutting, chest-forward corpulence, same natty button-up sweater with leather elbow patches. Same ponytail and round glasses. Same aura of lordliness and easy manipulation.

"Guitar," the man says, putting out a red, fleshy hand. "Don Guitar."

I reach for his hand, eyes darting around for the barkeep.

"They don't make the Go Faster anymore," the Albert-lookalike continues in his inimitable voice. "They don't do much around here anymore that would tell a person this place has history. Mind if I make a proposal to you, a little pitch you'd be the man to judge?"

I tell him to go ahead.

"First, allow me..."

He reaches over the bar for a bottle. Johnny Walker Black. He widens his eyes in my direction and I nod as he starts talking and pouring.

"You ever hear of Branson, Missouri?" Don Guitar asks.

I look blank while sipping my whiskey, neat.

"It's a small town in the Ozarks where some old hillbilly stars built themselves some bars and theaters. Started playing there instead of the road. Figured the crowd could come to them instead of them going to the crowd. And you know, it's working. Starting to draw some *real* stars.

Guitar paused, put his elbows on the bar in front of me.

"I'm thinking it's about time someone did the same thing for rock and roll. Here. Here in our little bit of heaven, halfway between two Woodstocks. Between Bethel and the majesty that is Overlook."

Hell if I know what got into me as the man talked but, all of a sudden, I'm laughing myself out of my seat. Liquid-out-the-nose bursts, spewing scotch all over the man mid-sentence. I sit on the floor and laugh so hard the tears swell my eyes.

"Heaven, you say?" I squeal, roaring into heaves.

I hear a chair squeak, a door slam.

I look up to an empty seat where Don Guitar had sat.

"You want another?" says a bartender lady with the look of a young Imogene Coca. "And while you're at it, you want to take this call? They described you to a tee. Said whatever you're drinking's on the house."

I take the phone in hand with a long, drawn out "Yessss..."

On the other side is nothing but a blank tone.

"What's with all the fucking phone lines going dead like this?" I plead to the bartender. "Is it just me or is something wrong here."

She smiled and shrugged.

"Sometimes you just got to go to who you're trying to reach," she said, sweetly. "Has anyone told you yet that you're dead, man?"

12

Klokko made his move out from behind the battered shopping center. He roared the Olds into a steady school bus-stuttered afternoon stream of traffic, anonymous and unnoticed. Pulled into the first gas station he could find that advertised a full-service option. That was the ticket, he figured. He'd worked in a gas station once and had the trick pulled on him. Guy stays in the car, asking for this and that. Windshields. Oil. Hell, check the transmission while you're at it. Then a fast pull out and back into the flow of traffic before the attendant can react. So you lose a gas cap.

Klokko had wanted to be bad because it was bad men who got girls. His brother had started to go bad. Pa was bad. If he was bad, just once, he could change. Be new. Find the love he'd wanted and jump the fence into that world of heroic song he'd long pined after.

But now on the edge of such a precipice, it felt different. *Real* bad.

Sure, his father had an edge. That must have been how he'd got his mother to fall in love with him. Wooed her out of a desk job in the county seat, college-educated and career-minded, up to his parents' place on Mt. Calvary. Then onto the back seat of whatever car he was driving at the time. Took her and, in the only act of goodness Klokko could recognize, married her when she got knocked up.

Klokko wished he'd had the chances, the normality, of others' lives. He might not have been so shy his head spun, so prone to blushing his name changed. Maybe Gerard wouldn't have died so young, caught by his own sad need to be bad, like dad. Good got you nowhere but unseen. Scared. Hell.

He remembered the sorrowful and pained times. Everyone had it better. Others had televisions and nice cars, store-bought toys, and birthday parties. He had bits of wood, old pots and pans. Too much time sitting in old cars parked dead behind the falling barn. He'd stand at the edge of the forest, dark wilderness stretching for miles. He cried over the bloody carcasses Pa would pull back each autumn when hunting season started with a scary dawn fusillade.

Klokko'd listen for something to make a strange sound, which he would imitate back. He could keep this up until a skunk or grouse, a white-tailed deer or gnarly, ancient crow would appear. Once he summoned a bear.

He wanted to warn them. Stay away. The world's nothing but death! You need song to live.

Klokko figured if he couldn't speak with fellow humans, he'd make friends with fauna. He'd summon and deal with that which scared him.

Pa would whip him good if he talked, as if any word meant "talking back." He got whipped when Gerard would act up. Gerard, his father would say, didn't need forceps to get him out of HIS mama, hadn't almost killed her with HIS birth. Gerard, he'd add, wasn't a "scaredy-cat mama's boy" like Richie'd always been.

Later, after everyone started dying, Pa stopped calling him Richie. Took to calling him Klokko like all the others.

Book bags like the other kids. A lunch box. Thirty cents for a hot lunch. Chocolate milk. There had been so much he wanted. Simple things, he told himself. Gerard grew bad but drew everyone's love anyway.

Klokko remembered the one time it seemed kids asked to be his friend. They came to where he sat on the edge of the forest making bird and animal sounds.

"Wanna play?" said Ronnie Mays, the buzzcut leader of the group. He'd been the first to touch a girl down there, the first to report what whiskey tasted like, and always the first for detention because of his smart-ass mouth. But everyone loved Ronnie Mays, especially the girls.

"Guess so," Klokko replied.

"C'mon then," Ronnie and the others said. "We'll go up in that two-story garage then. Your ma or pa around?"

Klokko told them they'd taken Gerard to town shopping. Said he hadn't wanted to go.

"Why's that?" Ronnie Mays asked. Klokko shrugged.

He followed, hands a-pocket. Not wanting to let on how excited he was to have been asked to play. Not wanting to blush.

Inside the barn's cool darkness, Ronnie lit a match, then a cigarette. He looked around at broken cars and car parts, old furniture.

"Got an upstairs?" he asked.

"Up the ladder," Klokko replied, motioning with his head into the darkness. Above was a square of dim light.

"C'mon then. Let's play us some cards," Ronnie said, leading everyone up the ladder to a low-beamed attic where the boys sat in a circle. The Mays boy brought out a Bicycle pack, started dealing.

"Game's straight poker," he said, a nine-year-old acting 30. "Strip poker."

Klokko could no longer remember the game itself. All that stuck with him was the chill he felt, getting more naked. And then the embarrassment when the boys took his clothes and threw them down the ladder. Ronnie Mays held him as everyone went down, whispering something about how they just wanted to see if he had a pecker.

After Ronnie went down the ladder, they pulled it away and ran off.

Klokko still hurt from that day. He'd sat there until dark when his parents came home. Ma called for him and he called back, quietly.

"Why Richie, why didn't you yell for us?" she'd asked, hugging the skinny, ungainly boy with the long neck and bug-eyes. She bundled him in the warm blanket with boats on it.

"I didn't want Pa or Gerard to know," he whispered back.

Later, Ronnie was the first he knew to die in a car crash.

A dark-skinned man with something wrapped around his head had come up to Klokko's window and asked him what he wanted. Klokko, still caught in the past, stared for a moment. He wondered if this could be an Indian. Like, from India Indian.

Then he remembered that he now had a plan. Time to execute, he said to himself.

"Fill it," he said. "High test."

The man, as old as his father but more methodical, bobbed his head like one of those back-window dogs he'd always wanted as a kid. Started filling the tank. Washed all the windows, smiling and bobbing his head every time he caught Klokko staring at him.

When he finished, he came up to the window before Klokko remembered what he was going to do. His plan to peel out fast into traffic.

"$18. Big tank, that," the man said in a sing-song accent.

Klokko stared, frozen.

"I've got no money," he finally blurted.

"No problem, sir. You pay later. I just need your name and address," the man replied, not missing a beat. "We aim to please here. New business. Are you..."

Klokko felt his neck straightening, his head gaining weight and its own sense of power.

"Not now," was all he could say, hitting the gas hard as he shifted into gear and pulled into a break in the traffic, eying the road ahead for likely side roads, possible escape routes.

Behind him, the Sikh shook his head sadly.

Klokko took a right at the first light he came upon, then another right onto a side street. He followed more side streets until one turned into a country road. He could tell by the mailboxes, the way the asphalt had been worn down, the burn of bottoming-outs at whatever rises came along.

The sky started filling with late afternoon color. He figured he'd find a hideaway where he could sit out rush hour and await the moon's arrival. It would be an orange one tonight, he figured. It was waxing.

Klokko pulled onto a major highway, no traffic in sight, and proceeded down a long hill into a valley. Up ahead he saw a bridge and a big sign. He crossed, eyes watchful.

"Welcome to New Jersey," read white on green lettering. "The Garden State."

"Uh-oh," Klokko said.

The cat purred as they entered deeper into New Jersey.

13

"So what if I'm dead. I'm still buying. Still drinking," I answer the Antrim's barkeep, back bar lights softening the dull sheen from distant windows to cast a pall on both of us. "If anyone calls asking for a man like me again, just tell them I've gone fishing."

Asked whether the caller was a guy or a doll, the 30-something smiles sweetly. "Both, honey. First one and then the other. You need a place to keep your sorry self tonight?"

"Besides the cemetery?" is my comeback. I feel a trouser wrinkle straightening out.

"Just tell me one thing, mister," she continues, not skipping a beat. "You keep up with yourself? Ask the hard questions? Just consider this the start of something. Answer any way you want."

I'm speechless. I take a long sip of scotch. The bartender watches.

"You come in talking to yourself and pour a drink, thinking I'm not watching," she adds. "I've had my eye on you. I know the score."

The woman hands me a towel.

"Clean your mess," she says.

"What is this place?" I ask, mopping something out of my beard. "Two-headed fish...what's with that?"

"Some say it has to do with the trout that's been drawing folks to this place for generations now, and the Junction Pool over there. But that's just Opening Day, almost a month away," she answers. "Ever since I was a little girl and came down with measles, I've been seeing double. Some who are here, some gone already. I've seen your type before."

I ask what she means, and she turns her back.

"You've got some lessons to learn, bud," she says, as I look into my hands where I'm fumbling with change. I want to pay up and move on. "You still have some traveling to do. Beat it."

Before I can come up with a rejoinder, she's gone. Vanished. The lights are out. It's cold. I head back the way I've come in, temporarily blinded by the shimmer of white light off Junction Pool beyond my car.

I turn back to the Antrim's door, but it's padlocked. Fuck all this dead talk, I'm thinking, as I head for a gas station and get filled up without the kid taking my credit card, yet again.

I've been dead before. Dead to my dad, dead to my brothers, dead to the world recovering from this or that. I've woken up thinking I must have done it this time, waiting for the grim reaper to appear before me. Spent hours, tripping, wondering whether I was gone. Or thinking myself alive, reliving a memory replay of what it was in my last moments forever and ever.

Dead my ass. I'm driving. The old Route 17, four-lane to one side of me, river to the other.

Dead tired is what I am. Maybe I can get past this weirdness with some *real* sleep. No more car napping. A bed seemed right, even if it was mid-afternoon by my reckoning.

I see a motel just ahead. I pull up and knock. Wait in the March air, hopping foot to foot and rubbing hands together for warmth.

Someone pulls ajar the punched-in hollow core door with the burglar chain lock still hooked.

"It's too early, sonny," says an old lady, slightly bearded and groggy eyed as if she's been awoken, or pulled away from marathon daytime television watching. "Try back in town."

"What town?" I ask. "I just came from there. I was at the Antrim."

"It ain't open yet, not for another two weeks," she said. She nods to the west. "Head up that way. You'll find something eventually."

I roll down the highway past boarded up homes with trailers in their yards, a few closed gas stations and convenience stores, a tire dump.

I pull over and step out of the car, surprised by the sweet-smelling warmth in the air. I've been driving too long. I'm in what may have been a town at some point. Two stop signs, bullet-riddled, with a streetlamp flapping in the breeze. Rusty squeaks beneath a roiling sky. Tall old clapboard structures in need of paint jobs. Spent neon signs announcing rooms for rent and cold beer.

I try the only place with a light on, even though it feels run down, disheveled. Hey, aren't we all these days? I pull the heavy door open and walk in, ring the bell. Nothing. I walk down the hall to a bar. No one. I listen for sound and hear voices and some music. Splashing. I head down another hall that smells of mold and chlorine. *Take A Letter, Maria* (Nice tune. Nicer guy.) I knock at a lime green metal door.

"C'mon in. Ish open..." slurs a woman's voice.

A large, naked woman is lounging in an octagonal wooden hot tub, her white breasts floating on the water's surface. Around her are three younger men with unshaved faces, grinning ear to ear.

"Whatcha want? Cat got the tongue?" she bellows. Bubbles burst the surface near her tits and the three guys giggle.

"Meet the fucking roofer crew," she says. "Whatcha want?"

I ask about a room.

"Too late, asshole," she says, reaching for a bottle of Boone's Farm Strawberry Hill. "Don't hit your butt leaving, dickless..."

The dame looked familiar. I don't want to know why, or from when and where.

I try the next place. No lights on, locked door. Peering in the windows, I see nothing but stacked tables and piles of rags.

I start back towards the car, slipping now and then on patches of ice in shadow, sidestepping slush piles. I spot a sign on a staple-studded lamp post.

"Searching out the perfect get-away? Look up, up and away...to the Owl's Nest," it reads.

I glance up the street, overlooked by a tree-dense mountain. Lights twinkle above the trees.

"Sure, we can accommodate. Always do," says the gaunt, bald-headed barkeep a few minutes later. He's shouting over Hendrix' version of *Like a Rolling Stone,* played loud. Place is empty except for the two of us, each wearing black.

"Room 666," he adds, tossing me a key.

He must have caught a passing look from my face.

"Just kidding. We got six rooms, and you got the last of 'em."

His voice is a growl; one of his eyes looks dead.

The song ends and restarts as I walk into a grand, heavily carpeted lobby and up a flight of stairs. I want to turn and ask HIM if I'm dead or something, but leave it be. Sometimes things simply repeat themselves like they have to.

The room's nothing special. Small windows, considering what would have been a pretty decent view. I turn on the tube. One local station out of Binghamton with a poorly coiffed lady talking about the weather. A badly flickering porn station on UHF. A test pattern. I leave it there, turning up the static to match my mood. I pull the curtains.

I look at the bed. It's been a while since I left the rumple of that Quality Inn motel room in Winter Park for the shower, losing Dawn and everything else in the mix of things. But first things first.

I wash my face with cold water. Poke a finger into my mouth to wiggle some teeth. Remember how Bob had once talked my ear off about how one's purity shifts to ambition and then strips one of all that's pure. How you start mixing up whatever you've created with your life, forgetting where one ends and the other keeps playing. In the best of circumstances, that is. That was the same day, in Manchester, where some asshole yelled "Judas" from the audience, and we later laughed about it.

I wonder: Am I a Judas? Or worse, could I be like the Singing Nun, found hung in her bathroom in Belgium. A year later and everyone still mystified.

I sit on the bed and dial Woodstock on the room phone.

"Hello," I hear my boy's voice, starting to crack from approaching puberty.

"Junior, that you?" I say, losing my own voice. "It's your father..."

"Hello, hello," I hear the teen repeat, talking into a void on whose other side I sit.

"Junior, Junior, it's me. Your father," I repeat, feeling a life of tears stream my face. The line hangs up and I just sit there, head in hands, static growing louder all around me in this place called the Owl's Nest.

What have I done, I cry to myself. What is this?

I need a pick-me-up. I wash my face a second time and head out from my limbo.

"Name your poison," the bartender says above the still-repeating Hendrix racket. "Snake Bite? Dirty Mother? Long Island Iced Tea?"

"How 'bout a Go Faster? You know that one?" I ask, seating myself on a barstool and searching for my reflection in what I had thought was a mirror behind the bar.

"Know it? It's all anyone drinks up here anymore," the barkeep replies. "Nothing like a Go Faster to get you moving slow, like one should. Need anything else while I'm at it?"

"Give it a moment," I reply.

I take a sip of the concoction I may have invented. Vodka, Grand Marnier, and about ten other spirits. Yeah.

When the Hendrix song starts in for a fifth play, I figure it's time for a new request. I lean in close, the bald barkeep mirroring my move.

"You wouldn't happen to know where I could get some, uh..."

The guy, face in mine, winks and grins, quickly finishing my sentence in a conspiratorial whisper.

"Hi C, health with a capital H. Try my friend, the doctor," he says. "Mister Twister, the doctor of Close Hollow."

"How'd you? I..."

"We're all of a similar shade up here, my man," the bartender cuts me off.

He hands me a hand-scrawled map.

"You'll get your beauty sleep later..."

14

Klokko worried about Beatrice. He'd have to make a stop for her. Soon. She needed food more than he did. She needed water.

He needed sleep.

Klokko thought of the way music had proven the saving grace of his life. At first, there were the songs his mother and grandma would sing to him. *Swing Low, Sweet Chariot* and something about a *Bye-o Baby*. Later, while he nestled in the back seat of the car with his blanket, something came on the radio. *Dream Baby*. Then there was something about a letter getting returned to its sender. And another about a sunny afternoon. *Yellow Submarine*.

Music jelled, later, when he was at the county fair and heard *Satisfaction* blasting out of a game booth. He wandered over in the direction of the music. A toothless carny turned in his direction.

"Two throws fer a quarter," said the hairy guy, all face-stubble in a tee shirt and blue jeans.

"What's the song?" Klokko asked, in a voice like he was dream-talking.

"Somethin' on the radio's all I know. Some English pussies," the carny replied.

Klokko nodded his head and shut his eyes, letting the sound of the song and its bitter lyrics fill him now, while driving. Men came on the radio telling him no no no.

"I don't mind if you listen, kid," the carny had said, just as Gerard had found Klokko and whisked him back to his family before trouble took hold. "Don't get yourself hooked."

He opened his eyes as something darted across the darkening road.

The Delta 88 roared by the Delaware, on the opposite side from where he'd been earlier. Houses were boarded up. Fields even more fallow than on Mt. Calvary. Just the sort of thing Pa always railed about.

"But *I'm* going to get to the bottom of all that now," Klokko said, the sound of his own voice surprising him as much as it did the cat.

Klokko stopped the car mid-roadway and listened to the clean hum of his engine running on a rare tank of high test. He reached over and patted the cat, then drove fast into moonlit stretches of road where he could turn the lights off and glide.

"I got a record player when I was 12," he said as the cat sat up. "I bought *Hey Jude* at the Ben Franklin's in Middleburgh. Got it memorized so I could use it like a timer when I got bored. 7 minutes and 14 seconds. Saved up for *The White Album*, which Ma helped me with. It scared the both of us, especially *Revolution Number Nine*. Then when *Don't Let Me Down* came out I thought it the most beautiful thing I ever heard. I had my first crush then, on Elaine Dameron, and we held hands on the bus for a week before she slapped me in front of everybody. I never knew why. I played that song over and over again for a month."

Tears streamed Klokko's face. He cried for the fact that he was talking as much as for the memories he was talking about.

"I have a father, you know," he said. "My mother and brother are dead but my father, he's alive. I have to find him."

Beatrice settled down, rubbing against Klokko as the blanket slipped from his shoulders and he sobbed with the clenched sound of a hurt dog.

The last inkling of sun disappeared into the western hills. He sluiced carefully through another town, staring straight ahead and not making a sound until he found himself by the river's edge once more.

Pulling by the side of the road, he turned the Olds' lights off and cut the engine. For a long time, he just breathed, very quietly, in and out, in and out.

As he sat in the quiet of the deepening darkness, nothing but the dripping of the March thaw to remind him there was still a world outside his head, Klokko slipped into one of his classic rock and roll dreams. He was on a stage filled with the smokiness and chemical burn of dry ice, music pounding around him with no discernable beat or melody. Ever so often, he'd see a fleeting glimpse of a rock star he recognized; a frizzy-haired Dylan or stone-faced Bill Wyman. Rick Danko sexy-plucked his bass guitar, then seemed to slip into liquid.

Klokko was groping. He was naked, a microphone in front of him. The audience included spotlit kids he'd gone to school with, girls he'd had crushes on, priests and ministers and teachers and gas station attendants. Ma and Pa held up Gerard, bleeding from the crash wounds that killed him.

His voice caught. He felt an electric shock waft through him. Klokko shut his eyes in the dream.

When he opened them, he was on a beach, waves lapping at his feet. It was a large lake but all the trees around him had died. He saw his mother and grandmother repeated in various stages of their lives, naked, their mouths open as if singing. Yet all he heard was that whooshy bottle wind sound from Mt. Calvary, accompanied by the light pitter-patter of sleet on a frosted window.

He wanted to force himself awake. The feeling became frantic. Something had happened. Someone had died. Same as when Gerard was found, a day late, headfirst in the oldest hemlock in Stony Kill Clove. Or when Ma spent her last hours in the hospital up in Albany. He'd been in this dream before.

Klokko opened his eyes to total darkness. Beatrice purred beside him. There was no one he knew well enough to be affected by their death, he figured. Unless he was being pulled to Pa for such a reason.

Klokko reached for the radio to see if something had happened in the wide world outside his head when a car's lights passed behind him on the main road. It made a U-turn 100 yards away and sped in his direction, whirling blue and red lights flashing.

Klokko listened as the siren moved past him, like something heard on one of those old quad systems. He turned the lights on, catching the Delaware to his left, then continued along the River Road. He passed into another town, wary. People were walking down Main Street, even though it was late. He saw a bridge crossing the wide river to another town. Saw a sign pointing ahead to Washington's Crossing. Klokko headed that direction, drawn by his mind's image of the nation's first president, upright in a skimpy but solid boat breaking through wavy ice to sail us all into a new future.

"No music, precious Beatrice," he said, voice measured and calm. Something had started to shift deep within. "Let's just listen."

The cat purred.

He followed signs and pulled down a hill toward a narrow bridge. Suddenly, his neck straightened before his mind registered what he was seeing. A toll booth. And half-hidden behind the booth, another cop. Young-faced middle-aged guy with a buzz cut.

Before his head could spin, Klokko spotted a parking lot next to the booth and U-turned, spraying gravel along the way. He raced back in the direction he'd come, eyeing the sides of the road for escapes and hoping that other cop he'd seen earlier wasn't also headed his way.

He knew, without having to see, that the sheriff's deputy would be up onto the same road coming after him and that, soon enough, that other cop who had passed in the other direction chasing some other poor driver would have turned back around, pissed. He was trapped.

Beatrice gakked, hungrily.

Up ahead, on a bend, a paved road headed downhill toward the river. He'd have to take it.

He crossed a one-way bridge over an old canal and sailed down a road parallel to that he'd just been on, moving the opposite direction. He saw the cop car up above and pulled onto a dirt pull-off where one could load a boat into the Delaware. He jumped out of the car as he saw the cop's lights turn down his direction.

"You mind, now," he whispered to Beatrice as he slipped out of his blanket and the door simultaneously. "Gotta go…"

Klokko clambered, naked, down into the icy river and found his footing in the muck and rocks of its bottom. The cop's circling lights moved to where the Delta 88 sat, still warm. A second cop car followed it in. He heard doors opening and closing.

The water around Klokko rippled as his neck lengthened like some taut water snake. He held his breath as the two sheriff's deputies turned flashlights on, trigger hands on their holsters.

"Now you hold it right there," one of them bellowed. "Get back up here, son. No need to run."

The cops inched their way in incremental steps to the side of the car, peering into it with quick, careful glances. By the time the first had gotten to the driver's window, the second, in ready stance just behind and to the left of him, seemed to relax.

"Well, what do we have here," his voice softened. "A widdle pussy cat all hungry?"

Klokko sank his head into the flow of water he was holding himself steady against. He opened his mouth and drank, silenced his mind against the cold coursing through him. He slowed his heart beat the way he'd learned years earlier, when his father would come into the room, eyes blazing, and his best option was to feign deep sleep.

He started singing "Hey Jude" to himself underwater.

"Look how cute she is," said the lead cop, reaching through the open window. "How incredibly cute..."

15

Lizzie, Pa, Dawn, Joe, the boys in the band...everyone's been right about me. I'm a fuck up. I start doing the right thing, fully prepared to take my life into my own hands for once, instead of leaving it to fate, or my addictions...and here I am following my nose up some godforsaken back road in the stream-roaring rush of early March thaw. Drawn by the C. The way's so narrow there's nowhere to U-turn without getting my wheels stuck in a ditch, and my rent-a-car teetering over the edge of this excuse for a mountain.

I've fucked up again. What's it matter if I'm alive or dead?

Could this, finally, be what the old guy was speaking about? The end of my mystery? What all the folks I've stumbled on in this journey were pointing toward? Denouement, I think the word is? The end, as Jim Morrison sang.

It's a longer drive than I expected, especially given how long I've been running since the last time I slept in that South of the Border parking lot. I check the crumpled directions in the seat to my right, alongside my lyrical steals.

The turn-off's by a waterfall, and only paved for a hundred feet or so. I can no longer tell the time of day, whether it's dusk or dawn slipping by as the sky shows color through the trees rising up either side of me on this mountain, several ridgelines away from where I'd started. I sense myself rising above treeline. Off in the distance lies the reflection of a reservoir, the glow of small Catskill towns and hamlets. The passage of time.

The Hamlet of Rock and Roll? Fuck me. Maybe what they were really meaning, all along, was simply my fate to end up as nothing but the most tragic of figures. Like these small communities that no longer rank as villages or towns that are lucky to end up on anyone's map.

I'm fated to play out someone else's drama I can do nothing to avert.

Not that I'm taking any action other than driving.

I pull into a field and, following my instructions, honk three times. Just down the hill, behind a stand of picture-perfect birches, a light turns on. It flickers three times and I get out the car.

By the time I've shut the door there's a tall and gnarly gray-bearded guy with pop eyes and big teeth standing beside me. All arms and hands. Blonde-white hair headed skywards. These strange, unreal white teeth.

"You look just like I expected you to be looking," he says, extending a hand and speaking in an educated rasp of a voice. His eyes pop wide for a moment. "You probably don't remember me, but we've spent time in the same rooms, you know. I probably don't look much like you'd expect me to be looking, if you can catch my drift."

He's turned and started walking toward the light in a wobbly scamper-like run, as if the recipient of countless injuries. Yet he never stops talking, not a beat.

"We got what you want, of course. Finest grade. Finest of everything up here," the guy's saying, leading me onto a path of glittering stones through the birches. His house looks to be constructed of nothing but windows.

"I used to be a lot closer to Woodstock, back in its day. Lived down the road from you at several points. But I like the view from up here much better. Air's cleaner," he rattles on. "And wouldn't you know, I've lost none of my clientele except what one would expect, given the goods. Town's aging. The whole culture is. The big money'll be in old folks' homes for old rock and rollers, if you ask me. One for the Dead Heads, another for the aged metal freaks. Rappers get their own village. Et cetera et cetera, my man."

We enter a room heavy with incense and the low sounds of Gregorian chants. The lighting inside is darker than what I'd been expecting. It's as if the sun's never shone in this place.

The good doctor motions me to one of two Adirondack chairs on a plush oriental carpet. I settle in, relaxed.

"Fix you a special cocktail?" he asks. "Word has it you're dead-tired. Been on the road too long. Making for the big change."

He's standing before me with a copper tray holding two small, gold-dimpled glasses. They're warm to the touch.

"Ginseng fizzes," he's saying, disappearing again as quickly as he appeared. "How about some fine French cheese and water crackers? We got a lot to get to here and not long to get through it all, my friend."

As I sip a warm mixture of vodka, sake, and root that tastes bitter yet soothing, the spectral dude hands me a tray of hors d'oeuvres.

I place it on the table and, reaching for a bite, feel the strap slip around my arm.

"We do things nice and easy, here," the doctor's saying as the needle enters with an inviting slide I've not known in some time. "Myself, I prefer acupuncture these days. The more, the better. Nothing like lying in a dark room stuck like a porcupine, knowing that one move and you're in deep, deep trouble."

I feel myself nodding into pillowy softness.

"This is my body broken and delivered that you may not repeat my sins, or my glories. This is my blood, shed for forgiveness and a belief in the power of rock and roll. Oh Lord, we do not forget your plan of salvation and the awesome signs of your second coming, when you shall reward all according to their deeds. We beg you for mercy and offer you forgiveness," runs the doctor's chant as I slip away, sailing on my blue ship into a darkness studded with the celestial lights of perfect high-dom. "Lord, you open our mouths and lips, sanctify our souls and bodies and free our minds and consciences so that we may call upon you, oh merciful one so high..."

It's winter, 1968. I'm outside the St. Moritz on Central Park South, shuffling through all those scraps of paper I used to have on me. Song lyrics on napkins, phone numbers on matchbooks. I'm in a pay phone at the corner of Sixth Avenue.

I struggle for a second, wanting to get out of this memory.

"Holy things for the holy with perfection, purity and sanctity."

I reach for the music outside me.

"One holy Father, one holy Son, one big old holy ghost..."

I'm wearing black corduroy ankle-hugging Lees, my favorite Filson jacket. I find the number I was looking for in an Ondine's matchbook and pop the nickel.

"Hey," I say, cool. "I'll be over in half, eh?"

There's frozen piles of sooty snow creating obstacles around the street corners. March weather, ever-changing. Like now. I pull my crumpled fedora low and head into the hotel, iguana boots clicking as I go. In the lobby, I pop into the florist's and tap a foot while this elderly man gets an order of chrysanthemums put together. I eye the girl he motions forward to take my order: fresh permanent, decent make-up, mid-to-late twenties. Probably lives in one of those all-women virginal hotels hoping to land the right husband. I smile, take off the hat and give a half bow. The girl blushes, wary.

"Yeah...you got black roses?" I ask. "Cute weather, eh?"

"All we have is red, sir," she answers.

"Red's fine," I say, thinking I'd seen black roses some-where...maybe one of those foreign flicks the chicks liked. What the hell. Color of death.

"What the hell," I laugh. "Three dozen. No card. Lotsa petals, y'know."

The girl turns and enters the glass sliding doors of the flower closet.

"Blessed be the name of the Lord," runs a litany of chanting tenors. "For he is one in heaven and on earth. To God be glory..."

I open my eyes and smile when the doctor takes the drink from my hand. I don't feel where it's spilled onto my leg. I shut my eyes again.

I'm riding with some kid in a monkey suit to the upper, gabled floors of the hotel, trying to look like a statue. Glance away enough to get the goon looking my direction, then dart the head back around so you can see his eyes shift back into place like a pinball sliding down the hole.

The doors open onto an oak-paneled vestibule with two doors, one right, one left. A handsomely tanned man in a black silk Nehru jacket, white jeans, and purple chukka boots rises and asks my name. "Jim's inside, waiting. End of the hall," the bodyguard says, opening the left door to a tastefully wallpapered hall lit by table lamps. "Great roses!"

A bout of heavy coughing from where I'm headed. The hall's muted, dark, shades drawn. I enter a large room filled with a rubble of trunks, clothes, a guitar or two strewn about. Everything's tilted—paintings, chairs, old gothic crucifixes, couches. Someone attempts to rise from a velvet club chair pressed in close to a bottle and glass-strewn coffee table but gives up after a brief struggle, waving a hand in the direction of the couch.

"Brought you flowers so you know I ain't queer," I announce. "We can play with the petals..."

"Whatever," mumbles the man in the chair. "My fuckin' ass itches."

He's shirtless, slumped back in cruddy leather pants and fence-climber suede mod boots. Dark brown hair unwashed and unkempt. Two-day stubble.

The stench of sweat, cigarettes, and hash overwhelms the scent of the roses in my arms.

The doctor says something through the haze, and I feel my wallet go free.

I succumb to the rose sweat of the St. Moritz.

"You bring your half of the money?" Jim Morrison grumbles, hand pawing his face. "How's it goin?"

"Cool. Contract shit. Nothin' like buying flowers to check out the female talent in a neighborhood," I answer, tossing the roses onto a pile of clothes in a nearby chair. I flop onto the couch as Morrison pulls forward, eyes on the roses, hand reaching for scotch. I shake out two glasses and hand them over.

"Roses?" Morrison says, breaking into another coughing fit. "Gimme a drink..."

He downs what I hand him and leans forward, hands scrambling around through the coffee table mess for a cigarette.

"Shit, man, people putting big money behind you; you got a part to play. You don't get high; you don't produce what they're payin' you to produce. You don't act the star; they can't be no fan. It's a fuckin' circle," Morrison intones, running his hand through his hair and coming alive with the swig. "Besides, you're in for a real treat today. You're in for a REAL high."

I pull out a pack of Marlboros and shake a couple loose, handing one to Morrison. He pulls out his Zippo.

"No problemo," I say. "So, where is the dude?"

"Don't mind the guy," Morrison replies. "Man's a pro. He says he's showing, he shows. This is the industry, man."

He rises, tugging at his pants to keep them up. Button's popped. He tosses me a wad of tin foil and stumbles across the room towards the far hall, mumbling something about piss time.

"Yeah, man. Sorry 'bout..." I mumble.

"Sorry 'bout nothin'," Morrison yells from down the hall. "Get that shit in shape. Have another drink."

I unfold a wad of rich, black opium from the aluminum, search the contents of the coffee table for a pipe, finish my scotch and pour another.

"Pipe's by my chair," Morrison yells. "Check the chair."

By the time I light up, Morrison's back in the room, dripping water. "Fuckin' roses," he says. "You're a genius, man. You're the Hamlet."

"Genius..." I sing to the tune of "Georgia."

Morrison picks the goo ball off the table after I hit on the pipe. He rolls it between his palms.

He fashions a spiral coil, a poised, hooded cobra that he places amidst a clearing within the roses. He picks up a long stem and starts slowly pulling petals, dropping them onto his chest and abdomen, sunk back into the velvet club chair.

"Fifteen minutes, man..." he says. "Epiphanies await, my friend."

I've got something to say.

"Jim, man, there's this girl I know. I gotta talk about this, man. Been on my mind."

Morrison, still wrapped up with the roses, grunts approval.

"I met her a few years back, like, when she was nineteen. We were gigging regular up in Toronto at the time. She's this model, see, beautiful. Her parents are professors or something. She was a ballet star back in Europe, y'know, when just a kid. Has this great accent. We went out back then. She's the best..."

I want to tell Jim Morrrison about Liz. I even want to tell him about my kid, even though I'm years from that. But he's lost playing with rose petals, looking into his lap. Finally, he motions for a cigarette and I shut up.

"Plan it right, man," Morrison growls, dragging on the Marlboro, its hot end lighting his face. "The key's the money, man. Don't you see that? High maintenance women have high maintenance needs. You're an artist. You need her like you need what's coming in that door in a few minutes. You gotta make *her* need *you*..."

Moving in my chair I feel a slight rush of air. Must be the elevator, I think.

"We believe in one God, The Father, the Almighty, maker of heaven and earth, of all that is seen and unseen," Morrison chants in an otherworldly voice. "We believe in the son's rock and roll eternally begotten of the Father, Rock from Sex, Sex from Death, True God from real Highs, begotten, not made, one in being with the Father because through him all things were made. He came down with all the power of the Holy Ghost the two of us will come to embody, man, born of the sweetest virgin, suffering so we can finally know the truth of death and burial. On the third day, dude, we're going to rise again and climb mountains and we will judge the good shit from the bad and our kingdom, man, will have no end..."

I hear a door open and close. Morrison stumbles up and heads toward the sound, hitching his pants up and running a hand through his dark mane as he continues his benediction.

"We believe in that fucking Holy Ghost, all the shit we're given about fathers and sons. We believe in one great motherfucking explosion of creativity tied up with good sex, good music, and the best drugs money can buy. I look for the resurrection of the god-damned dead, as well as the life of the world to come. Amen."

Jim Morrison swings the door open shouting, "Mickey! How's it going!!"

Sitting atop some mountain in the deep Catskills in a quack doctor's chair—March 1986—I feel cold air give back to warmth. It's like I'm getting folded into a womb, a perfectly heated bath.

For the second time this night I feel the wakening flow of tears on my cheeks, running towards my beard, my neck.

And for a moment, at least, pure silence.

16

Klokko heaved a sigh of relief as he rumbled over the steel bridge back into Pennsylvania, vowing never to visit New Jersey again. That was too close a call even if he felt cleansed by his baptism in the chill river.

He was even heartened by the sweetness of the two cops, who didn't even bother searching for him beyond a fast flashlight sweep of the surrounding trees and riverbank before splitting.

"Maybe I've been wrong about some things. Maybe there is a goodness to people once you scratch the surface," he said. "The songs, they only tell part of the story. I should try my own hand at this writing stuff."

Beatrice nibbled at the bag of cat treats the policemen had left for her, alternating with laps at the water in a hubcap that Klokko had brought her from the river.

"Sometimes," he went on, "You just got to wait the bad times out. So, I sit in the river a full 57 minutes and fifteen seconds. Happy? I am."

He had watched for lights another 24 minutes and 42 seconds, getting the warmth back in his bones after nestling back into his car, his blanket.

"This must be the witching hour now, Beatrice," he said. "The moon's rolling down to the ocean, following on our tails like a big old orange."

New Hope's Main Street was awash in light. Empty. He turned north, eying the restaurants and inns for a dumpster. Made it all the way up to another toll bridge before turning back. Finally, by an old stone house between the canal and river, he saw what he was looking for. Several cats lingered by it. That meant something fresh.

Klokko pulled the car into a spot along the narrow street, behind two others.

"Let's not draw any more attention than we'd get anyway," he said to his furry companion. "You stay here now."

As he shut off the Oldsmobile and listened, Klokko thought he heard live drumming. Deep bass rhythms and a flute. But it quieted as soon as he shut the car door to stand still and listen more closely.

He wrapped the blanket tight around himself and started down a dark side path and over a footbridge towards a quaint riverside restaurant. French. He'd seen pictures of places like this. For the first time he could remember, it felt good to be in a town, even if he was sneaking through it, naked except for his baby blanket.

Klokko aimed for the dumpsters, shooing cats away and looking in all directions as he quietly, slowly lifted first the dumpster cover, and then himself on tippy toes to its edge for a peer in.

"Jackpot," he whispered, reaching for a crusty baguette and a head of lettuce. He placed the gathered food into a pile by the dumpster and searched a bit more, finding half a salami, some chunks of cheese and an almost-perfect tomato. He quietly shut the dumpster and, looking all around, inched past the restaurant to the riverbank. He settled his night eyesights on a grassy spot beneath picture windows, overlooking the bridge he'd just crossed and the New Jersey town of Lambertville across the Delaware.

Quietly, quickly, Klokko started eating. He was better used to canned goods, much of it left in the house from his grandpa's hoarding days back when everyone in rural America was ready for a Communist invasion. But this stuff wasn't bad. He gnawed hungrily at the bread, alternating bites of cheese and salami. About to bite into the head of lettuce he heard something. A giggle?

Klokko's stomach gurgled. He resumed attacking the lettuce head. Heard something again. A splash and another giggle. His neck stiffened.

Just downstream, also in the shadow of the stone restaurant, sat a group of figures. He rose, very slowly, ready to dart for the car, a salami in one hand and a baguette in the other, a rind of cheese between his teeth and the blanket wrapped around his waist. The lettuce rolled into the river with a plop.

"Dude," came a deep young voice from the group. "It's cool. You want a sip of wine to polish that shit off, man?"

Klokko was ready to run. Then a girl's voice chimed in.

"Don't be scared. We were diving earlier, too," she said as his neck started relaxing. "We're doing drum circle. Come...it's warm over here. You need another blanket?"

Klokko stood where he was, not used to being addressed. He reached down and rewrapped his dead mother's tattered blanket around him tightly.

Someone started a rhythm on bass conga. Someone else beat a tenor bongo. Four or five instruments later, a dirge-like rhythm established itself and the girl was inching, in the shadows, toward him, half dancing, half swaying to the music in her puffy orange down jacket.

"It's okay, hobo man," she said. "We do this every time the moon's out so sweet and orange."

Klokko stayed still, like a deer.

"I'm just traveling on. Don't know these parts much," he heard himself saying. "I got scared there."

He nodded, in the dark, across the river.

"New Jersey scared me," he continued.

"Dude, it scares us all and we're from there," said the deeper voice. "Join our circle. Drink some wine. You must be freezing, dressed like that. But it's cool..."

Klokko started to shake his head. The girl's face moved into the light of the moon for a moment. She was dark haired. Frizzy, like that girl from camp.

"You know which way Philadelphia is? I'm looking for a place called bala...Bala Cynwyd," he said, deeply and solemnly. The tenor of his voice felt strange to him.

"Just follow that road there," deep voice replied.

"We'll ride with you if you want" added the girl.

"I'm kind of scared, and quite a bit unprepared. Can't take all of you," he replied, hugging the blanket around himself. "But my car's warm and you'd like my cat. I've got some great music..."

"You've got a car and a cat, dude? We're there," said the guy.

"Here, let us help you with this stuff. Harry, you get the wine and smoke. Tell the others we'll see them tonight."

Klokko thought about the two—she called herself Santa, a name he'd adored, like rock and roll, since childhood—as he started to fall asleep later inside a stone teahouse inside the walled garden they had led him to outside Bala Cynwyd. That was after they'd all squeezed in together up front in the Oldsmobile, singing along with the tapes they kept pulling from Klokko's collection.

"I don't talk much," he'd told them as Santa petted the purring Beatrice in her lap and Harry smoked a cigarette, wind from the open window blowing his long hair around his handsome face. "I've talked much more than usual today. We'll talk later?"

He dropped them at a train station in a place called Manayunk. Santa had wanted to go down to South Street for breakfast. Check out the scene. Klokko said he couldn't drive there; he'd have to start back soon.

"What you looking for, dude?" asked Harry, who'd stashed his bag of drums and instruments in the back seat of the Olds.

"I thought it was love," replied Klokko at the station. "Then I thought it was my father, who disappeared a long time ago."

"That's deep, man," said Santa, shuffling her feet. "I wish you luck and give you *my* love."

She kissed him on the cheek, and he blushed.

"I blush," Klokko said.

"We see, dude," said Harry. "You be good, now. Whatever you were looking for, you seem to have found something better."

"You take care, man," added Santa.

"You know, I've got two dads. I'm trying to move beyond them," interjected Harry, speaking over his girlfriend as if she weren't there. "Get some clothes, dude."

"Must have dozed off," Klokko thought, waking in the teahouse later. A crane of some sort padded through a lily pond in soft morning haze. He watched it step ever-so-slowly forward, head tilted to the possible movement of fish and frogs. He felt as peaceful as the bird, and almost as patient. Something had moved deep within him.

He had been dreaming, again. He was riding an owl out of this walled garden, celestial voices rising as he ascended, looking down at his Oldsmobile, presumably with him still in it driving, making U-Turns in a suburban neighborhood, seemingly lost. He rose higher until the entirety of the East Coast came into view like a living map. Only Florida was floating away, severed, and sinking.

He opened his eyes, gathered the old blanket around him and started to make his way back to the car.

Harry and Santa said the place was a museum. They'd been sneaking by the place for years. Her father, an artist, had had a friend who'd worked there. The place carried a medieval air about it, stony and heavily timbered. It felt like the sort of place he'd been placing his chivalric ideals in.

The young couple had shown him where to climb the wall. Pointed out the teahouse.

"Look, the moon's hiding in the reeds," Santa said, her head in Harry's lap.

"I better get to my business," Klokko had replied. He had a long drive ahead of him, many more adventurous challenges to overcome if he was to make it to Winter Park and find this Dawn from his dreams. Maybe even Pa.

But as soon as he'd dropped them at the train, and Harry had mentioned all that about him looking peaceful, Klokko decided to come back to the garden. To the magic teahouse.

Walking back across the edge of the lawn following his cat nap, Klokko felt rested and powerful. He heard the sound of a choir and stopped himself. The music was coming from a series of high windows in the wall above him. He leaned his back against the stone and listened until the chill turned to warmth and the sky brightened to a dull purple.

"I could have been a museum," he said, *sotto voce*. "But I have my own life now."

He was no longer certain he wanted to continue this journey. What was before him no longer felt like a grail, but a mirage.

Klokko felt strangely happy as he listened to the sounds of morning in a city. Beatrice meowed as he clambered into the Oldsmobile. He drove in traffic with his father's shades on, figuring everyone else was in their own world here. No one would notice him. And what, really, was there to notice outside oneself, anyway? Klokko laughed at the thought of this new level of comfort, as strange a feeling as his dip in the Delaware. Or his first real conversation with strangers since the photographers and their writer friend.

At a stop light he turned on the radio. Usually he sped-dialed away from any evangelist bullshit, but the bible banter seemed to fit the scene. He turned it up.

"And the Lord said unto Elisha, do you know that today I will take away your father? But Elisha's father said to his son, 'Don't worry for I shall never really leave. Just ask what you want of me.' And Elisha said that what he wanted most was a double share of his dad's spirit. His father said it would be so, but only if the two could shake on the matter, which never happened because a great whirlwind came, something like what we know as a tornado, and whisked the father up into heaven. And, oh my, but the son cried then. 'Father, oh father,' he wailed. 'Why have you forsaken me,' and he took hold of his own clothes and ripped them from his body, then ripped them further into shreds. And he reached down to the cloak out of which that tornado had sucked his dear old dad and he took that for his only garment, to cover his nakedness..."

In the Main Line suburb's pre-rush-hour traffic, Klokko's old Olds looked out of place, ancient. A tattered relic. A bum. But its driver, the naked man himself, clothed in a tattered garment like Elisha, didn't mind. The story he was listening to, for once, fit the scene that was unfolding all around him.

"Later, when Elisha fell sick and prepared for his own death, his son Jo'ash went to him and fell to the ground and wept, 'Father, oh father, my father. The whirlwind approaches. But Elisha told him to get a bow and arrow and face the fates. 'Open the window and face back to the north,' Elisha told him. 'Make your own battles...'"

Enough, Klokko thought, and he reached for the dial. He immediately recognized the first song he came upon, just not the cracked version he was hearing. It was *I Shall Be Released,* the old Bob Dylan and Band classic. Only the voice singing was older, more ragged, almost crying. Just a piano accompanied the tattered voice.

Klokko pulled behind a parked car and put the car in park. He had to sit back and listen. He knew this song always moved him to tears.

Sure as shit, it did yet again.

He also knew that his original plans were nothing. There was no reason to go to Florida. Forget Dawn. Pa.

He was naked in a city he didn't know.

He wanted to get back to his mountains, his own sense of an overlook.

17

I come to in darkness. I'm alone. No doctor. No drugs or other paraphernalia. No Gregorian chants.

I stumble to my car and notice a band of brightening in the east. I drive downhill.

The high felt good but this isn't my mountain, isn't what I've been looking for. I need coffee. Should I head back to the Owl's Nest for the rest I need and paid for?

How long since I stepped out of that Winter Park shower? If I *am* dead, I'm in pretty good shape for a dead man. No rigor mortis. No stink or maggots crawling out my eyes.

I need to talk to my mother, way back home. I want to see my brothers. I need to speak to my father, even though he's long gone. Time to play my own role as a dad.

I sit in the car. Turn the heater on. That memory I'd started on from the St. Moritz rushes back...

Enter Mickey Twist—smooth as silk, impeccably dressed, elegant as a single malt whiskey—into that disheveled hotel room. Into the next ten decades of my fucking life. Sandy-haired, blue eyed, dressed to the nines in a camel-hair polo coat with belt-ed back and paisley silk scarf, tan slacks, and freshly shined Church's penny loafers (without the pennies).

He knew me instantly. Commented on my Filson. Called me Hamlet.

The guy knew all about opera and ballet yet could talk of what gun to use game hunting in the Transvaal. Had fly-fished the best streams, skied with Killy, hobnobbed with the Astors. He knew the Ivy League, what it meant to be Social Register.

"I'd just LOVE to meet your friends," he said. Morrison, getting a fresh glass for the man, tossed in a quick something about getting a finder's fee as I ogled Twist's look.

"Just call me Mickey," he said, shaking my hand with one of those warm power grips that seals the fates of nations. "James Douglas," he added, turning to Morrison. "Stay comfortable."

"Woodstock? Love the place," Twist went on. "Spent a great deal of time there hanging with the theater crowd. Love the Maverick. Rented John Flannagan's studio one summer. Bought some art..."

I wanted to start into my theory about rock being the young classical music. All I remember, in the end, is making him laugh. Morrison, too.

I drive right on past the Owl's Nest turn off. I don't need it anymore. I'm going home.

"Listen, Jim, you mind if I talk straight here?" Twist said after a few minutes of cultured chit-chat back in the St. Moritz all those highs ago. "Your friend here seems afraid. Mind if I straighten this mess out?"

He smoothly turned towards me.

"Richard, you've got $10,000 on you. You've never made a buy like this before. You're new to the business. With your background playing bars, on the road, you've never dealt with the big time."

I tried opening my mouth, but Twist raised a hand.

"Hear me out," he said, as smooth as a parent lecturing his errant child. "You're thinking narc. You're thinking, 'I don't know Jim that well. I don't trust his success. You mistrust his being from Los Angeles, a town you've only passed through and are feeling nervous about having to record in next month. The fact that you're living upstate in Woodstock tells me you're a bit nervous about this city, not to mention those like me who are born and bred to it. Do you understand me? Am I right?"

Leaning back in his chair, Twist re-crossed his legs left to right.

"Well?" he asked, smiling.

"I wanna be careful," was all I could reply.

I pull the car over and shut my eyes with the memory.

"Listen," Twist continued. "The first thing you learn when you succeed in what I do is realize that it's never the cops you should be afraid of, it's other dealers. You see, all you have to worry about is money. My worry is double that. Triple. I deal with the cops. I deal with the other dealers. I deal with the record companies, who end up paying my fees in the end because they know my value to the very ideal of artistry. And fourth...I deal with you and people like you. Like Jimmy boy, here."

I open my eyes. The car is at a strange crossroads, dirt roads in all directions. I pull out and head down a hollow and up a short hill. Thoughts move me through the landscape decisions. I feel like I'm singing.

The sky is full where I'm headed. Just get me to Woodstock, I think. I'm needed. And I need.

"So, friends, can I offer you both a taste of what we've been discussing here?"

Twist walked over to his polo coat and fished out a folded manila envelope. He extracted a tightly wrapped baggie pressed white with sugar-brown grade A Turkish heroin.

"Only the best for those I trust," he said, pulling out a mono-grammed handkerchief to wipe away the rose petals for a clear surface.

I notice my fuel light. Got to keep an eye open for a station. But then I settle back into this latest in a string of memories I need to work my way through if I'm ever to get back to Woodstock, let alone up that mountain my whole rotting body seems destined to be headed for.

"Gentlemen...your enjoyment," Twist said with a smile, spreading his arms in a gesture of supplication.

"Not joining us?" Morrison asked, a straw suspended above a series of lines.

Twist shook his head. "Business, my friends. I've got to meet my fiancée for skating and hot cocoa. Can't be late; her aunt's accompanying us to *Aida* tonight."

Up ahead I see a station. Not open, yet, but I can wait.

"Watch the ice," I'd yelled after Twist when he left that after-noon. He'd taught us how to count out wads of hundred-dollar bills using a breath method. Hold it in and count. When you need your next breath, you've passed the thousand mark.

"What the fuck you doing, man," Morrison said as soon as we heard the elevator whoosh south. "You want to insult a man like that? You want to get us both cut off, man?"

I apologized, noting how nice Mr. Twist was, what a good businessman.

"Nice?" Morrison snarled. "You kidding? Mickey's a celebrity dealer, one customer at a time. He leaves me, he's got others in line to take my place. Wanted you because he's thinking he might hook into six noses through your one monstrosity. He works for the record company, man. I wasn't kidding about that fuckin' finder's fee."

After a pause, staring down at the rose petals, Morrison spoke again, quieted.

"I got to tell you something. If you eat the right stuff, keep yourself in shape, change your blood every once in a while, you can live forever."

An old truck pulls up to the side of the station and a red-faced man in his seventies gets out, lanky in overalls and glasses, a "Sid's Ford" trucker's cap on his head.

"You been waitin' long, mister? I'm Sid Ford. Usually in by now but had some extra breakfast," he says as I rustle awake. "Just pull her up. I'll turn the pump on."

I feel the sun reflect off an opening window across the roadway.

"Jumpin' jiminy," Sid says after opening my tank to fill it. "Sounds like you've been riding on air like some dead man emptier than sin...."

18

The strange version of *I Shall Be Released* that Klokko, parked with the engine running at the edge of North Philly traffic, was listening to, came to a sudden end. A smooth voice came on talking about what a sad day it was, what with its singer's death.

Klokko gripped the steering wheel. Could Dylan have died? He realized he hadn't thought of the songs as ever having been populated, lived in, and hence able to be left by their singers. He felt tears.

Beatrice rubbed against his blanketed legs.

"I'm going home, sweet thing," he said. "But first to Woodstock. There's a house I want to see."

It wasn't the big legend that was gone, but that other guy. The hairy Canadian dude in that band that had been associated with Dylan. The one from Woodstock. Richard Manuel.

Klokko rubbed a palm against his eyes then pulled onto the side streets of suburban Philadelphia. It was time for people to start emerging from houses to stand by roadsides awaiting school buses. Fathers were getting into cars to go to work.

Instead of hiding, shrinking into his seat from fear of his nakedness, Klokko rode straight through it all, looking forward. Like a Richie. Like some guy wrapped in a blanket because his name was Richard and that's what he had to, wanted to, be doing.

A young boy waved from beside a stone garage. Klokko raised his hand in reply and smiled coolly from behind his shades, like a rock star.

A little girl waved from a group of kids. He smiled.

By the time he'd pulled onto a main avenue, Klokko was waving to everyone who waved at him. Then waved at passersby, who seemed to smile every time they waved back at the strange looking man in a blanket and dark sixties-style shades driving by.

It was time to be a song, Klokko thought, getting into this radio thing, these talking voices, for the first time in years. It was really something, life with reception.

He pulled onto a highway. Then onto an Interstate. The kids from New Hope had given him cash, filled his tank. Said they dug his vibe and wanted to help him out, the way he'd helped them. It was karmic, they said.

"Karmic," Klokko said. He repeated the word several times as Beatrice gakked beside him, well fed on cheese and salami.

He pointed the Delta 88 north. Followed the signs.

Klokko shifted around the FM radio dial. Moved from classic rock to soul, from oldies stations to New Wave songs he didn't know what to make of. For a while, headed inland up the Pennsylvania Turnpike, having opted out of a return to the state of New Jersey, he settled on AM talk radio. Began cursing angrily at what was being said about affirmative action and pornographic artists, without understanding what he was angry about. Finally, he decided he was angry enough to get off the highway and head back to New Jersey.

That was the second toll he approached in a day. But this time he took his ticket with a smile.

"Fuck Ma, fuck Pa, and double fuck my brother Gerard," he hollered in the midst of 80-mile-per-hour traffic on Route 1, passing Princeton. "Fuck my teachers, fuck the President, fuck the Pope and fuck you too, God," he screamed, straining his already well-strained vocal cords.

He shifted the dial fast through songs, none catching his wild new mood until he found something super-fast and kind of crazed, all about some girl named Sheena. A punk rocker. He hit the steering wheel in rhythm, jerked the car around with the melody. Beatrice scampered under the seat.

When the song ended a young girl announced that she was just in one of those moods.

"Right on!" Klokko screamed. "Just one of those fucking moods!"

She went on to say she was just going to keep playing Ramones all day. Who cared, anyway.

"Who cares anyway!" bellowed Klokko, his neck taught, bobbing to the "one, two, three, four" that started the next song, and then the next. "Fucking Ramones!"

He traveled with the station a full hour. When he hit the radio-blur of the Ramapo Mountains, Klokko got his own rhythm going, beating on the steering wheel and undulating his head like a snake under a snake-charmers' spell. The car lurched and sped.

He turned the radio back up for Springsteen's *Hungry Heart.* Pulled up close behind a slow-moving Lincoln with an older couple in it. Almost kissed the bumper as its inhabitants kept checking their mirror to see who was riding up on them. The woman turned. Then cowered, seeing Klokko, naked, sunglass-hidden, his head bobbing like some creature escaped from her nightmares.

"Everybody. Is. NAKED," Klokko screeched, window down to the Bruce as he passed the oldsters in their Lincoln.

He automatically checked all directions for cops. Safe. The sun was reaching its stride overhead. Must be closing in on the Thruway, he figured. We'll be in home country, soon.

At the Kingston exit, Klokko steeled himself for the toll booth, a twenty in his hand. He turned off the radio, wrapped the blanket back around his nakedness. But the interchange was much easier than expected.

"You look warm in there," the older, friendly-looking man in the booth said, taking his ticket and the money. "Here's your change, sir."

Sir!

"Thank YOU, sir," Klokko replied with a smile, sunglasses off now, the cat meowing at the man from his side.

The toll collector smiled.

In this new mood, riding his unexpected confidence and good cheer with nothing but the radio, now playing endless songs by The Band in memory of their departed singer, Klokko decided he should head back home. Or at least up to Sid's Ford and his beloved's home across from it.

It was Saturday morning. No school bus coming for her. She'd likely be home, where he could watch her from across the road. No. He'd walk across and up onto her porch. He'd knock on her door and say hi to Bobby Mason and nod her direction when she asked who was there. Bobby would invite him in, and they'd talk of old times and he'd insist Bobby, and the girl, call him by his real name. Richie.

Klokko thought again of the singer who had died. Didn't know what he looked like, but the news had made him cry. Why was that? Was there something undeniably human, like blood or breath, like spirit or that thing everyone called soul, which flowed through songs and words and the like, connecting everyone the way bones connected a person and kept him from crumbling to the ground as a bloody pulp?

He heard that song about loving a girl who didn't know she was loved. The one about being in bad shape but not caring. Another about crossing some great divide. Whole albums' worth of songs.

Then he escaped the radio signals and entered back into his receptionless Catskills.

Klokko was speeding in on Sid's Ford and his love.

He slowed and made a sign of the cross over himself, another over the cat. He started making one in the direction of the service station, his girl, the places he'd grown up in, his house at Mt. Calvary. But then he stopped himself.

"Fuck you," he whispered to himself. "Fuck you all."

He screeched to a stop right in the middle of the highway, throwing Beatrice up against the dashboard.

"Fuck you. My love is just love. Fuck you, Bobby Mason, for all you done to me," he yelled. "Pure love. Fucking pure fucking love. That's me."

He reached over, pulled the cat up from the floor and placed her back on the seat. Petted her. He U-turned and took backroads up towards Mt. Calvary, feeling fresh making his way without aid of rock and roll for a change. He pulled up the rutted driveway to his rotting house, put the car in idle and grabbed Beatrice by the scruff.

"Sorry, sweets," he said, the cat looking at him wide-eyed. "Something's come over me. Mission time."

He opened the dark kitchen door and tossed Beatrice inside. Didn't wait to hear the "Gakk" he knew she'd make. She'd fend for herself.

Should he get clothes?

No, he decided in a flash. I'm my own man now. New clothes will just have to find ME now.

"Someone else's story, that one," he said. "I'll follow this one to its end, I will."

Back in the still-warm Olds, he continued driving by instinct. Roads that knew no traffic but for him.

Klokko started beating out a dirge-like rhythm on the steering wheel. That rhythm those kids had been playing by the riverside.

"I'm going, going, going now; I'm going to my love," he chanted. "I've got to go to Woodstock, now, to see my man 'bout death. I been there once, been there twice. Went with grandpa then my daddy's dead wife. I'm going now, going down to my new new love. I'm going, going, going now, down to Woodstock. Down to death…"

What would he talk to his love about? Love. But then what would he talk to Bobby and the girl's mother about, Klokko asked himself?

He'd tell them about his adventure. Hell, his wearing only a blanket would be enough to start, even stop, *any* conservation. He'd talk about this dead rock and roller and what his death meant to him. What music means to all of us. He'd talk about what it had been like, growing up as he did. His search for his Pa. The tragedy of Ma's death. Gerard's.

More importantly, Klokko figured he'd like to listen, even if it was only to hear Bobby Mason and the girl's mom tell him how fucked up he was for showing up at their house on a Saturday morning wearing nothing but a tattered baby blanket.

Maybe he should turn back? It wouldn't be much to get some clothes, even if only to wear them just long enough for him to get something new to wear, pulling some money from the jar he kept in the boiler room.

Off in the distance, Klokko saw the sign for Sid's Ford. But then he felt the car slide some.

He noticed the road was covered in slugs. He'd heard of this happening near the creekside at times. But to see it real? Sure wasn't pretty, Klokko figured as he slowed down.

Then he noticed something else unexpected. A black car at the pumps in front of Sid's, across from his love's home. And Sid talking to some bearded hairy guy in sunglasses just like those he was wearing. And wearing just the sorts of clothes he'd just imagined himself buying.

For a flash, Klokko thought he might have entered another dream state, what with the slugs and this version of his inner self up ahead of him.

As good a reason as any, he figured, to U-turn yet again and get back to Plan B. Besides, if that was a dream him at the pumps, talking to Sid, why not let him get his girl warmed up, and her ma and Bobby feeling all peaceful and stuff, while he prepared his own return.

He surprised himself, feeling no fear, no jealousy.

"I've got a right to sing the blues, a right to shout out praise" Klokko sang/ranted as he started back towards Mt Calvary. "But I've also got the right to get beyond all this crap everyone's put in my head, all over my stinking life. School, parents, death. Fuck you, death."

Klokko felt strangely exhilarated, strong. Like he could drive all day and night...not for her, or anyone else, but for himself alone.

"For me, man," he said. "I write my own songs now!"

Turning onto the dirt roads he'd been driving since a kid, Klokko laughed to himself. He saw a skunk crossing the highway and swerved for it, pinning it with the bumper and watching it roll away in somersaults before it had sense to spray.

"Ah, my pretties," he said in a movie cackle. "Life's just like that in the rearview."

He was coming up on the crossroads where he'd earlier seen two owls.

"Ready to run the yellow jello," Klokko whispered like a madman.

Just as he started across the four stop signs, giving them no heed, an old man appeared in the middle of the road wearing a button-up sweater and chinos, a trucker cap on his head. He shimmied to the center of the crossroads and calmly turned to face the car bearing down on him fast.

Klokko screamed on the brakes, stopping inches short of the old man.

"You crazy fucker!" he heard himself screaming.

He noticed the cap on the guy's head.

"Stand Back," it read.

19

"They'll be getting up right around now. Jessie Ketchup's what people call her. She put ketchup on everything back in kindygarten, back in Sunday school, you name it. Some say it was to make up for her dad being gone and all, raised by just her mom. Jessie Ketchup's true as heaven, truer than hell. Pretty girl, she is, too. Real pretty."

Sid Ford's talking a mile a minute as I turn back towards the sun. I slip on my shades. Don't want him to see the yellow in my eyes.

An old car starts to pull in as we stand there, Sid talking and me listening. But it quickly U-turned and headed back the way it had come, squishing slugs as it went. The old man shook his head and opened his mouth as if to tell me a whole new story related to the green Oldsmobile and its driver.

"What's with all these slugs?" I ask, unable to get my eyes off the slimy exodus going on as the day warmed to something more than the usual thaw, as if a door to Hades had been ripped open. Some had made it to the highway's double yellow line as if trying to escape the fate of what remained in the road edges' shrinking soot-snow patches.

"They do that every once in a while. Gets really bad in summer, and occasionally during one of these early thaws. Never seen it quite like this," Sid explains, starting into a long description about why slugs crawl onto asphalt in the first place. A natural death wish, like porcupines licking the bottoms of cars, getting after the sweetness of transmission fluid. Or gnawing on houses painted with toxic paint.

Looking at his oil-blackened hands, then up and over his shoulder towards the open bays of his garage, I'm hit with memories of my pa. Ed.

I'm a slug. What have I done with my life? I've been a fool and, worse, a dangerous fool. I hate it all: Mickey Twist and Jim Morrison. Bob Dylan and my place in The Band. Beatles and Stones; all the music. I hate rock and roll and what it has done to us. I hate this fucking geezer yapping at me in a high-pitch monotone about goddamned slugs.

I've fucked it all up, but good.

I remember the look on Liz's face when she first met Twist, looking on him the way I'm looking at these slugs. Mickey in a Jag, all smooth and talking just to her, all "misters" and "ma'ams" beside the Woodstock Village Green. Sun just perfect on bright October leaves. And she, gripping my hand in hers, her other hand on her pregnant tummy.

It was good she didn't see *my* look, like the one I'd just given the Ketchup girl. She'd have slapped me upside the head, then left me.

But maybe she did see.

"I've rented an estate by the Hudson and we're wanting you two. My sister's up with her kids this weekend..."

Lizzie squeezed my hand. How could she have known about who he was so quickly?

We *had* talked. I told her Mickey was with the record company. A&R. Artists and something or other.

"Tea and sympathy," Twist said with a smile, shaking our hands and scooting away.

For the moment. One of many.

"Is there a pay phone?" I interrupt Sid Ford. He says no but if I can keep it local, he'd let me use his.

"Woodstock's all," I say. "Gotta check on my wife and boy."

"Why, sir, that's just down the road, it is. Good hardware store, there," he replies, revving himself up for another high tenor lecture. "It's always good for a man to be checking in on family, especially when it's this time of the morning and that man hasn't, by the looks of it, been home in some time."

I walk into the station's crowded office, eyes open for a phone amongst the parts catalogs, calendars, pieces of this and that, and newspapers. When I spot a cord I follow it under a copy of the *Woodstock Times*, not yet yellowed like everything else in the room. It's old-style, heavily rooted to the desk. I try Liz's number. Busy. I try again, just in case I got it wrong the first time. It just rings, unanswered. Same thing happens a third time and then, on the fourth, it starts going busy again.

At least I'm no longer getting people treating me as dead air or some odd, unimportant ghost calling in from the other side.

"That's it," she told me a year or two into the routine that resulted from Twist's presence in town. "I'll restart my career. Move back to my parents with the kid. Make it in Woodstock on my own, if I have to."

"Like hell," I said, raising my fist in the doorway. "That's my kid. You're my wife." She slammed the door and locked it. How could I have ever explained that I just wanted to hit myself?

And so, she left. The first time. A second time, too. She'd come back after a few weeks. I said it was just the money, that it couldn't have been for me.

I try the number again. No answer. Instead, I dial The Bear, a number I've stored in my head since they opened.

My call gets picked up on the second ring. The voice sounds familiar.

"Sweetheart," I purr. "You know who's calling you?"

"You bet," the voice purrs back, game. "What's up? You got a call. Just a moment ago."

"Well tell 'em next time to leave a message. Even better, tell 'em I'll be meeting them there at the bar. Tonight. Make it eight o'clock."

"Make it six, fella," the voice replies with a laugh. "You read the papers yet?"

Out on the roadway, slugs crawl toward the other side. Some are making it. Most aren't.

The traffic outside's a jittery flow of mud-splattered pick-ups and older American makes from the 1970s and sixties. Every once in a while, a shiny milk truck rumbles past, squishing an army as they go. I keep thinking, half-hoping, someone'll slip, or get stuck like in that cartoon world where I used to go all Goofy-faced.

Jesse Ketchup comes across the road from her front porch as I talk on the phone. She's leaning against my car, speaking with Sid. She wears Capris and a Hello Kitty muscle shirt. The chill air lends her flesh goosebumps. Small nipples scream howdy. There's something familiar about her, just as there's been something familiar about everything these past days.

"Missy here says she has a question for you," Sid says as I approach. "You get your wife and kid on the line?"

I shake my head, looking out at the slick of slug guts, the sun catching it just so.

At the mention of "wife" the teen girl seductively raises a red sparkle-toed foot to scratch behind her calf and pouts.

"I seen you somewhere?" the girl asks. "You been parking out here across from my window, mister. Or are you just famous or something?"

Sid laughs and shakes his head, moving to open his bays.

"Kids," he mutters. "She asks this of every guy who pops through."

Jessie Ketchup reminds me a bit of Dawn. It's her attitude, that saucy way she has. A bad girl looking for a bad boy.

I also flash on the voice I just talked with at The Bear. Sounded like that Imogene Coca lady from the two-headed fish inn. Dead ringer.

"Didn't you hear me ask you a question, mister?" the girl asks louder, pushing her hands back a bit on the car door so her tits point my direction. "You as bad as them slugs."

"Maybe I'm a bit of both," I say to the girl, walking up to just inches from her sultry pose. "I was just talking to my wife. I may have been lookin' at things. And I might be famous for some of what I can do."

"Well, that's real nice" coos Miss Ketchup in reply. "But I'm just waiting for my school bus."

I could have hit her. It would be like hitting some sense into my own kid, my own sassy self when I was her age. Maybe a way of knocking Mickey Twist out of my memory. Out of my fate. Knocking everything back.

"I got a good-looking boy almost your age," I say. "You be careful now."

I brush my hand past her lightly panted leg and open the door to my car. She acts like she could have swooned, but then scampers away like a naughty 13-year-old, carefully avoiding the slugs in her way.

"Guess you're just famous," she yells over her shoulder. "Too bad you didn't learn nothing in school."

Instead of replying, I just shake my head, get in my car, and turn the ignition. I remembered that line.

I pull out, nodding at the girl. In the rear view, I see someone come out onto the porch of the house across from Sid's and yell in her direction. Must be her mom. From the way the man who comes up behind her moves, I figure he must be mom's special friend.

I stop, back up a bit, and roll down the window as Sid steps out the bay in my direction.

"Listen, I'm sorry about Jessie, but she being..." he's saying.

I wave a hand and tell him he forgot to ask for money.

"Oh, I figured you'd just be having a credit card and I can't take credit cards," he answered. "But you being from Woodstock and all, you'll be getting back to me. Everyone always has and hopefully always will. You hear about..."

"Thank you, Sid," I interrupt before he can launch another diatribe. "Listen, I was wondering if you'd finished that *Woodstock Times* in there. If so, would it be..."

"Oh, that's a humdinger of an issue. Just out yesterday. Already read it cover to cover, I did."

He scampered back inside and reappeared with the newspaper before finishing his sentence.

"Sid, you're a good man," I said as I took the paper from him, hearing laughter across the road as the mom's friend slapped Jessie Ketchup's rump as she climbed the school bus steps. "I'll be back here lickety-split."

I fast-rolled my window and peeled out as Sid started talking about how there'd been something he read that I should find interesting.

I nodded at him, tapping my ear as if to say I couldn't hear.

"Now that I think about it, the photo on the front page," was the last I heard. I was close to home now.

I had a lot of questions that needed real answers.

20

The man in the Stand Back cap had an impish smile. Without asking, he climbed into the car as Klokko pulled his blanket tighter.

"Thought you'd be able to give me a ride up to the cabin," the little guy said. "I'm just shy of a century, y'see, and the legs don't work like they used to. We'll be making a right turn here once she turns green."

Klokko looked straight ahead, rattled by the man's sudden appearance. He'd been on such a high and now it was starting to seep out of him. Why, he thought, did he let himself get into these situations?

He turned, as the man had requested, when the light shifted green.

"I'm trying to get to Woodstock," he haltingly said. "Need some things..."

"Good place, Woodstock, if also a bit odd. Lots of folk come up walking from there. I mean, most of them bring the car and stuff. Park it and then walk. But some actually walk," the old guy started chattering, making no mention of the driver's strange apparel, or lack of any besides the blanket skirted around his lap.

"It's that close?" Klokko asked, without self-consciousness for once. The guy hadn't mentioned his nakedness. Furthermore, he hadn't figured himself so close to his destination already. Had he always been this close? Perfect timing, given the fuel light had come on again. Should he ask the old guy for money? He'd spent what the kids gave him on tolls and forgot to get his change the last time he paid.

"Used to be I could walk everywhere. Didn't like the car and how fast it made you go," the old guy continued. "One time I came across a boy along here. He was playing with this water snake, see, who had its teeth in his arm. Water snake was hanging straight down off that boy's arm, blood dripping and everything. I told him I didn't think that was wise, carrying a snake like that. So I told him to take that snake off his arm, I did."

"I don't like snakes," Klokko said. "My mother didn't like them either."

"My Ma always told me they were pure evil, she did. Told me she burned out an entire forest when she was heavy with me. She'd seen one climb up out the hole in our outhouse," the old guy said. "One time, I saw this snake in an old chestnut tree. Thing poked his head out at me and flashed that tongue of his. Put his head back in that hole as fast as he'd poked it out. Right at my eye level, that was. Snake just kept poking in and poking out the whole time I stood there. Guess that's when I decided I might as well not be 'fraid of no snake, even if I didn't like them."

The Delta 88 rolled past the turn off that would have led Klokko home.

"You make your next left, a right, next two lefts. Even with that warning light you should have plenty to get you where you're going," the old guy said. "You drive these roads a lot but never past where you've always gone, I take it?"

Klokko smiled. It hurt. But only a little, he realized, keeping with the odd feeling. He liked these changes coming over him. They seemed easy now. Especially given all those years of fear.

"You listen to music?" he asked the old guy as he started over a mountain road with old farms along its sides, high mountains in the near distance. "For the longest time I was thinking music was key to all."

"Only the music of the wind and water, the rain and leaves falling," the old guy replied. "And the songs we learn as children."

"But what if some of us can't grow up like the others?" asked Klokko. "Or we have nothing else to turn to."

The old guy reminded him of Ma's father, who he used to imagine as his real dad. And yet there was also something in this old coot that was like his Pa, too. Something sad and try-hard.

"You got a radio?" asked the old guy. "I had one once. Seen a television, too."

Klokko liked the man. He talked, playful-like, the way all the old guys that used to be around when he was a kid talked. As if there was more time, then, for jokes. For a playful ribbing of the ways fate can catch us.

"I got hooked to music bad, y'know," he told the old guy, who motioned him onto a side road that got swallowed by a mix of forest and fields, then right onto a similar roadway with some turnpike name. "Love songs driving me crazy. Rock and roll…"

"Never could understand that stuff. All this caterwauling by skinny men who didn't really want to be around women," said the man, eyes keen to where they were going as Klokko listened intently. "I know it's been important, real important these last thirty years or so. That what's bringing you down to Woodstock, son?"

Klokko nodded his head. Maybe it was time to listen to what the old man listened to? Maybe try hearing what was inside his own racked body and mind a bit?

"You one of them Woodstock rock star types?" the old guy asked. "They're always in trouble, you know, look'n for ways to climb out of the messes they've made. Not able to be by themselves or with the women chasing them."

Klokko laughed. The old guy motioned him to make another left. They started climbing slowly at a crawl pace, the red empty fuel light temporarily going off in the process.

"I wish or, well, used to wish I was," he said. "Rock star, I mean. Though I guess you could also say the same for the girls. I've been too scared to ever do anything. I once sang at home but now I can't. I keep wishing that instead of having my head full of other people's words I could have a song all my own."

"It's a good thing, son," said the old guy. "You know they found a skeleton up here this week? Down by the Bridal Veil. Said it was a Woodstocker. Killed by a bullet wound, they said, some four or five years ago. Maybe longer."

He paused and clicked his tongue a few times, the way Klokko's grandpa used to do.

"And to think I walked in there all the time, year in and year out. Must have been a freshet that uncovered the poor fellow."

Klokko remembered how grandpa would take him into town for a haircut. They'd meet his old friends, all wearing hats and talking up whatever they'd read in the newspapers. No one ever mentioned the wives they'd lost. The sadnesses or missed opportunities of their lives. It was nice, Klokko thought, to escape his regrets. The songs. From now on, he vowed to himself, he would find ways to better appreciate the beauty around him. Everything else, he realized, was nothing but a form of death.

What was it about driving on a steep incline that opened up his thoughts and spirits so? He was glad he'd picked this old guy up.

"I've always thought the music soothed me. Kept me from hurting myself or other people," he said, alternating eyes from the road and the expensive New England-style and Contemporary homes hidden behind hemlocks, to the old guy, tufts of white hair sticking out from under his Stand Back cap. "I grew up surrounded by sinners. God-haters and seducers and batterers and diviners. I would try to figure out what it was that made them so, which just made me look deeper into sin until I started to hate God and want to seduce and batter myself. So, I listened to music. At least the music that seemed to be all about love."

"It's an omen when someone finds a skeleton," Stand Back continued, cataract-eyes looking straight at Klokko. "Means a soul's migrating. I seen it in trees and bird-folk. Seen it in the critters 'round about the time winter starts in on 'em. It's not necessarily anything having to do with that corpse that was found. All's I know is that the ones that gotta go start scurrying around, looking for some kind of nest. They pick up what's shiny, circle around a lot, then lie down for the next chapter. Trees...they get this quiet look to them, ready to give up the ghost on their leaves so they got the energy to make it one more year. Those that don't, they shed early."

"What's your favorite song, mister?" Klokko asked, pulling the car to a stop and looking right at the old guy.

"The one my mama sang me. About the chariots," Stand Back said. "Right up there with that other one without any real words, the one about saying Bye-o to the baby."

Klokko felt a twitch in his neck. But it was just a smile, again.

"What's your name, young fella?" the old guy said. "Mine's Jim. But some folk call me Cato."

"I'm Richie," Klokko said. "But some folk call me Klokko."

"You been here once before," Jim said. "You're gonna let me out in a moment and I'll tell you a good place to wash yourself in the stream. Just don't use no soap because it's bad for the wild things. You'll feel like you been *there* before, too. Because you probably have. I get off up there; my place is through the woods a bit."

They pulled into a weedy driveway with a gate crossing it, a trail leading uphill into forest.

"I'd invite you in, young fella, but I don't have nothing for you except some spring water from a metal cup. Better to drink it from the crick, if you ask me," Jim said. "And you've got things to do, I can tell."

Klokko smiled and reached his hand out to the old guy as he opened the car door.

"My favorite song's the same as yours," was all he could say. There were still others in his head, but none of them would mean much to the old guy, let alone in this wild, natural terrain. They'd mean nothing until he made his way to that pink place he needed, now, to get to.

"You pull off a mile down the road. You'll see a gravel area and a trail sign. Head in until the woods feel like a church. Then follow the sound of the water. Don't mind who owns what when you're there. It's all for the taking."

The old guy looked at Klokko like he knew the thoughts in his head.

"You'll coast down to Woodstock. Or *almost* all the way. Enough to finish your mission," Cato said. "And feel free to stop by the little church there if'n you wish. They're always welcoming."

"I just wanted to thank you," Klokko said.

"Thank the heavens. Thank nature, thank Hell," Jim replied, turning to shuffle into his woods. "And don't you worry 'bout that skeleton they found. That's some other sad story that'll get told eventually. None of your business."

The old man paused by an old clothesline and turned to the car one last time.

"It's one thing to listen to others' songs," he said, solemnly. "But then you gotta sing 'em yourself. Reverse is true, too, you know. Man can make 'em up but then he thinks himself a creator. You got some get-togethering ahead of you. What's split comes together. In and out, like that snake's tongue."

Before Klokko could answer, the old man had vanished. Had he looked down a moment and missed something?

The mid-morning sun rolled up above.

Maybe the shadows had shifted strange as they do in such mountains.

21

It would have been faster to follow the school bus to Woodstock, but I wanted some radio reception. Maybe I could get my hometown station, The Bulldog.

I take that long curve along the Esopus where the mountains peel back and twiddle the dial. Eureka!

"It's a sad day here in Woodstock, memorializing one of our chosen sons. The snow still clinging to the underbrush and threatening to fall at least a few more times. Yet the warmth is with us today, and sunnier days on the horizon..."

I recognized the smooth FM voice. A good man. But like all good Woodstockers, a voice in love with its own mellifluous tones.

All I wanted was tunes. I didn't want to hear what the DJ wanted to tell me.

"Folks are flying in from all reaches of the rock and roll globe for the Memorial Service in Bearsville this evening. Word has it Mr. Dylan, Eric Clapton, maybe even a Beatle or two will be there. Yet another sad day for rock and roll. But in its odd way, a catharsis."

Maybe I *am* dead. That makes me laugh. But also shake my head, what with the recent slew of such services in town. Albert.

"As the sweet man wrote once, so eloquently—and we'll be playing this and other songs by our friend all day, as we've been playing them the past two, 'Life's got so little to say.'"

Oh, heavens to shit, those are *my* words! I almost hit the roof of the rent-a-car and want to stop but I'm moving too fast.

What the fuck's all I can think and say, repeatedly, as I pull to the side of the road and stop.

They're talking about me on the radio. Could this be some joke? I push buttons, turn the radio back on and the same guy's finishing the same shit. All about me. Or at least someone with my name. With *my* music.

They start into one of my songs and I flip through the dial as my head races. I hit the tail end of an early song, our biggest hit, coming out of Poughkeepsie. And then another off that same album coming out of Kingston.

No no no! For God's fucking sake, no.

I turn the radio off and notice the grease-stained newspaper Sid Ford had handed me.

On the front cover's a montage of photos of me. Story says I died March 4. Hung myself in the bathroom of that motel with the fogged-over mirror. Had quotes from everyone there. Some stuff from Liz and Dawn about how good I'd been in the past year.

What the fuck? The question repeats. I got *out* of that shower. I'm here, headed home. I've been eating and sleeping and drinking and driving and singing. I've met countless folks and made it all the way from Florida in normal time. I can feel things. I have body aches. There's spit in my mouth, snot in my nose.

I wonder what would happen if I started the car up again, get it up to a good speed, and then took my hands off the wheel. If I'm dead already, would it matter?

I drive, catch myself as I roll towards the edge. Then catch myself a second time as I edge over the double yellow line with a green Oldsmobile racing towards and past me.

Must be some miracle. A second coming, like I used to be famous for. I was ready for a new life. Ready, finally, to change it all. I can't be dead because I feel the bumps in the road, the tears streaming out my eyes.

I pull towards the edge of the road again and scrape the bumper against the guard rail with a loud crunching of glass, plastic, metal, and stone. Sparks, man. It's living, bad but alive. I can hear my breath, the beating of my heart.

What does one do in such a circumstance? I'd had no training in these matters, all those hours of acid or speed-fueled midnight TV binges didn't prepare me for this shit nearly as much as I'd expected. Hoped. I recall several hours laid out on a picnic table in a Santa Monica backyard with a golf ball of hash working its way through my gut while believing I was in some emergency room trying to hold on after jumping out a window in downtown L.A. But *that* wasn't this shit on the radio, or that newspaper staring up at me from the passenger seat. I've spent my fair share of time in *real* emergency rooms, thinking I was just high watching teevee in my rec room, fire roaring in the woodstove, as they pumped my stomach. Brought me back to life.

I'm dead? What gives? I should be pissed, sad, unfounded, lost—and can see those emotions like that far-away dream vision I'd have as a kid in my sickbed. I don't feel connected to any of it. I keep thinking this must be a dream, a flashback, an hallucination, one of those half-real moments, maybe based on something I ate, or that H the mountain doctor shot into me in that glass house surrounded by birches. Should I try wetting myself to get out of this bad dream?

This sure ain't grief. Like the sudden sobs we all fell to when Jimi and Janis and Brian and Jim and Moonie and my Ma and Albert and my cats and Robert Plant's kid and Stan and the old dog Jess and all the rest died. John Lennon, for Christ's sake! That was like having something ripped from you, the room shifted, an unfunny bang to the funny bone. Hurt. That wasn't like everyone gone in the past year, from Orson Welles to Margaret Hamilton. Karen Ann Quinlan left to rot with her tubes pulled out and Paul Castellano rained with bullets in front of Sparks' Steakhouse. Phil Silvers and Rock Hudson. Donna Reed. Ricky Nelson, a sweet guy downed in a plane crash. Gordon MacRae, my onetime idol. Leon Klinghoffer pushed off a boat. The voice of Bullwinkle and Mr. Peabody. All gone. All disappeared forever.

This, in comparison, was unreal.

I can beat this rap.

I pull off the main road with an idea in mind. I remember a shortcut. Maybe that's what I need to do, like the old guy and others had been talking about. Head up through the mountains.

I scuttle along a stretch of road where the skies open. Old Catskills, not messed up yet. I cross a creek swollen into muddy turbulence by the warming weather's snow melt, then see a stream of parked cars. I seem to know the place and stop the car. There's a path leading through tall hemlocks into the darkness. I take it.

I'm looking for answers.

After a short climb I come upon a meadow. Patches of snow keep me stepping gingerly until I clear the trees, drawn by drumming.

When I see them, the rhythmic hippies, I drop low and edge the woods until I can get a better look at what's up. No one seems to notice me.

Out in the field's center, a dozen shapes move in rhythm, djembes, congas, bongos, and other percussive instruments. People in puffy overcoats beat on logs, rocks, their thighs, and chests. A slow, languorous, dirge-like rhythm, a low chant beneath it all. Three women undulate, sexy but sad, in front of a plume of smoke. The air is sweet with pine, pinon, and reefer smoke.

Someone walks out to me and hands over a fat joint. I take a long toke.

The kid nods somberly. Makes to reach out and touch me but pulls back, turns, and walks back to the circle.

There's a movement at its edges. A tall kid sluices behind the crowd, edging away as I start to mirror his movements. I could swear it's Junior so I move in his direction. The music surges, retracts.

The figure scampers across the meadow into hemlocks. I follow.

"Wait!" I yell. "Junior?"

All I hear, ahead, is a low whistle. Like breath over a bottle.

"Junior, wait!" I repeat, speaking full voice now, throat hurting as I do.

The darkness of forest swallows me.

In the distance I hear water.

22

K lokko sat in Cato's overgrown driveway a long time, still as a dead man. He wondered why Pa had left him. Would he ever return? He remembered, vaguely, a time when he was very little and loved to wrap his arms around daddy's legs. So long ago, that feeling.

Klokko wrapped himself in his blanket and listened to the soft wind rustle leaves and grass. He heard a bird sing. In the distance there was water running.

A dip into a spring would be nice now. Sure, he could use some clothes. But I'm here, Klokko thought. Not my father or my grandfather or anyone dead or heard on a recording. This is a new story. There's no hurry.

He re-started the car, engaged the transmission, and started back up the country road from Cato's house. One curve on, he saw the pullover, stopped, and got out of the car, wrapping the blanket around him as he started up the hill.

He realized his feet must have hardened. They felt no cold, no hurt from the shale pathway.

Klokko stopped and watched a bird land in a branch before him. A chickadee, alone. Silent without a partner. It seemed to look at him as he took notice of a singsong murmuring coming from a ramshackle chapel, all wood and shingles.

When it shifted to the singing of several male voices in unison, the bird flew off over the structure and into the hemlocks. He moved towards the chapel's stoop and slowly opened its heavy door.

"When the spirit is faint within, you know my path. In the way along which I walk they have hid a trap for me," three men chanted/sang in nasal harmony, each elongated breath holding in the air as steam when they inhaled. "I look to the right to see, but there is no one who pays me heed. I have lost all means of escape; there is no one who cares for my life. Attend to my cry for I am brought low indeed; a lamp to my feet is your love, a light to my path."

The space surrounding the black-robed men, all bearded with salt and pepper taking over their dark hair, was richly wainscoted but musty-smelling. No electricity, just the wafting light of candles and sun filtered through cracked stained glass. Small carvings of saints, Christ on his Cross, a shrouded beauty he assumed must be Mary, sat on small shelves. Another chickadee skittered beam to beam above the singing, as if trying to keep time with it, to join in.

Klokko thought of the red-haired damsel he'd been watching for months. She was but a girl. He was glad he hadn't gone up on that porch dressed only in a blanket and had left that other guy—his doppelganger—to deal with her.

"What have I done with my life?" he asked with a wail. But then he answered his own question. He'd survived two deaths and a disappearance. He'd kept clean and, except for his crushes and shyness and solitary ways, never really sinned. He'd never hurt anyone, unintentionally or with malice. He'd never raised any expectations of talent he could waste. His only fault had been to let himself be swallowed by others' accomplishments, others' dreams. The visions of teens.

He was prepared to mature. To become a man, at last.

Klokko shifted his gaze from the bird up above to the men in black robes facing each other, sing/chanting their ceremonies. All were his age. Their faces were filled with hope, but he could also recognize the residue of old fears around their eyes.

"As the sun reaches the midpoint of its path, extending its warming dominion, may your mercy, Lord, be upon us," one of them soloed in high tenor. "Now as the sun's rays envelop the earth, may your compassion be upon us. Accept now our praise and receive our prayers. Show us the way, dear Lord. Show us the way."

How can one start anew after 40? Burn the house down?

He would do two things, he decided. Give himself over to fate. But also clear away all that had *seemed* like fate to him. Shed habits, in other words. Forget loving others, one-sided, and open himself to others' love, even if it could never match what he'd spent a lifetime dreaming about.

Klokko straightened himself. Felt his blanket cocoon, as clothed as any of these priest monks in their black robes.

He could no longer imagine his neck stretching. His blushes.

"O Lord, the night and day are yours; you uphold the light and the sun. You are the father and the son. Through all your power you direct the sequence of the seasons," the singing continued.

Klokko tip-toed back towards the door he'd entered. He needed baptism. He had to start his new life.

"Be for us the day that never ends. In the morning, in the evening, at this noon hour in midday let your light shine in our hearts, enlighten us with the knowledge of your truths, your love."

He opened the door and stepped out as the rafters' chickadee swooped out over his shoulder and joined its mate. Bird love, he thought. Natural companionship.

Inside they started the Lord's Prayer...

"Our father, who art..."

He'd never been able to get its words straight.

He bowed to the chickadees then headed back down the path to his car.

23

I follow the sound of a stream. I want to jump in and resurrect myself, prove my middle-aged ass not dead. Even if, for lack of coffee, I *am* feeling like death warmed over.

Despite my public persona, based on the few songs I wrote, I've never been too keen about nature. Sure, campfires are okay for marshmallows and backlighting sexual hijinks. Who doesn't like a drink down by the river, or a joint on the beach? But mountain climbing, night camping? I can piss in the woods but don't try sending me out there with toilet paper.

Worse than the idea of me being dead is the fact that I'm wandering the Catskill forest in silk shirt, zip-up boots, and a skimpy leather blazer. I want to follow Junior, but I may not be ready.

I want the kid to know some things about my Pa, Ed, and Gladys, my Ma. We all really cared about each other. Same with all of us rock and roll boys, making sure to be calling family every time we could get to a pay phone sober enough not to start balling—or laughing—at the absurdity of our homesickness. We got weaned too early. You could feel the roots of rock and roll was nothing but a baby's howl.

I want to sit down with Junior, hug him long and say, "Son, you can't be doing as I have done, just as I couldn't do as my Pa did. I want to lead you to that next level up the mountain beyond all this. It's how a family grows, son. It's how we all get better, as a people, no matter the odds."

I also want him to prove I'm not dead.

Instead of catching his trail, though, I find myself lost in what at first seemed a scary forest. I roil about, stumbling over roots, bumping up against trees and branches. By the time I finally struggle my way out of the dark woods, I'm in a new meadow with an older copse of hemlocks and tall pines before me, sweet smelling with the sun shafting through it, catching life in each of its beams like an example of holiness.

Do my regrets mean I live? I hooked up with a good lady then fucked it up. Lived in Levon's garage, eating the man's food while various ladies fixed me. Kept telling me they were all mine, that I was still the greatest. That what I really needed was to get away from small town talk.

Someone got Joe to book us some gigs. Me, first, to see if I still had chops. And then these last months of middling gigs in half-ass joints.

All the while, I had another life, too. The one where I'd straighten up once a week to spend time with Liz and my boy, passing from an adoring puppy-dog-eye look to the practiced nonchalance of a true rock and roller. This made me proud. But then I wanted it gone. Why did I need I pull him down my road, after all? Where had it gotten me?

Maybe Dawn knew me better than I thought, figured out what was really eating at me. The constant homesickness that had been there since I was 16. The need to drown every sorrow that came my way. That feeling of being a Judas.

Did I hang myself as he did?

Could any of this have anything to do with whatever reason Dawn hadn't been in our Florida motel room? Why had the old guy said something about her being with Liz? Why the fellas wouldn't have minded me being gone? Why this whole shitty trip had been so goddamned strange, so filled with memories clouding in like crows coming at a dangly piece of tinfoil caught in a barbed-wire fence?

One fucking drink too many. Where had the doctors, the cops, the morgue, the fucking hearse been? Why hadn't I been privy to any of that, pray tell?

I should have written new songs when I could. They've welled up in me, at this point, like drowning tears.

Time lapses. Hemlock branches snap at my face. I push through the forest's edge, aiming for a place where the canopy grows high and cathedral-like and you can shut your eyes and picture deer lapping at clear, stream water pools. My feet are getting clogged in mud, so I choose to walk where there's still ice. I delight that I can't feel the cold.

It's one of those March moments where the sound is half-hollow with emptiness, half-filled with returning birds brushing through the upper limbs of forest. A chorus of dripping. Sunlight that speaks.

Ah, Dawn, Dawn... Afraid you'd run into Lizzie or my boys in The Band. Scared of seeing my kid because you said you didn't know how to act around anything that innocent. Told me once how you'd been scared of being a kid around the grown men God had designed your body to attract.

I just nodded along. All talent, after a fashion, is the same thing as that, I guess.

The sun's up. I'm in a clearing, walking on moss. The stream's nearby. Another time-lapse, I guess. The nature of death, I wonder?

There's a small waterfall, ten foot high, emptying into a boulder-bordered pool draped in hemlock roots and low-dipping branches. A couple patches of snow remind me it's not yet really Spring, and yet the scene feels warm.

I shed my clothes and dive in.

Instead of shocking me, the cool water feels soothing, the way a chill glove in winter can comfort an even chillier hand. I paddle around and find a place to stand and wash myself. I reach into the bottom and pull up sand and mud, rubbing the stuff all over, then rinse. I stand in the quiet burble and listen to the bird calls. I used to know such things. I *must* be alive.

Is this death trip a dream?

No matter how fucked up you get, you can always see that reaper's face grinning back from the mirror, that haunted skull under the face that's smiling. I could see it in Dawn's half-smiles. In the guys' faces whenever I finished a solo, no matter if it worked or not. I could hear it in Liz's voice on the phone. Hell, it was there in my own voice, caught for posterity on those half-dozen or so albums I actually sang on.

But that didn't mean I was gone, ashes to dust.

I dunk my head into the cold, icy water so I become part of its flow. It ribbons and snakes the long hair on my head, from my beard, like grass tendrils in the stream. I open my mouth and let the water eddy there, occasionally swallowing a gulp as I rise enough to breathe through my nose.

I try saying something I haven't said since I was a kid.

"Our father," I start, "Who has made art of heaven. Hollow is your name. You're going to come, as a king, and your will's going to get done. Please, God, give us some bread; forgive me my trespasses. Let me even forgive those who trespassed against me. I'm sick of being led into temptation. Please, deliver me from evil. Now and forever..."

I submerge my face and roar back up with a loud "Amen!"

I get out of the water and shake myself off. Haven't felt this good in years. I look down at my clothes. Fucking ugly 80's things. Where's my Filson and corduroys? What's with the pimpy, silk crap, the zip-up boots, the tapered jacket and skinny disco pants, anyway? Who am I, Mickey Twist or some strange made-up dude like you see at the edges of playgrounds, hanging around on the wrong side of town?

I start shaking side by side like a dog. I race through the soft-needled woods, barefoot and naked, whooping like a banshee. I run for what must be an hour, maybe two, finally coming to rest at the edge of a field, where I can see the road I've just been on and a green flash of car sailing by.

Getting down on all fours, I crawl slowly. I'm thinking it'd be fun to drive naked for a spell. Maybe all the way into Woodstock. Maybe right up to my ex-wife's door, the better to confront her and my kid. See if they think I'm dead, too. I end up on the edge of a dirt road, muddied and wild-looking, hands and knees scarred and bleeding. Before me rises a large clapboard structure draped in little flags. Weathered. A sole, droopy-paned old casement window is open. Inside is an orange-glowing and inviting room. I can swear I hear, very briefly, the low tolling of a bell.

Another new chapter? Do I enter, keep following whatever happens, or turn back, find a new way?

A bit of both, it turns out.

24

Klokko almost missed his spot. He parked behind a black rent-a-car with Florida plates. Must be one of those Woodstock walkers, he figured.

He'd been enjoying bathing in the beauty of the world, but a little physical freshen-up would be good. Klokko wanted to be ready for anything.

He got out of the car and headed into the dark woods. Followed the sound of water and, for a split second, what he could have sworn was some sort of joyous whoop. An "Amen!" The deep, high peak Catskills forest lightened the deeper in he got and Klokko recognized some of the trees on the edge. Hemlocks. Sugar maples and birch. American beech. And standing a bit by itself, scruffy and ancient, an old American Chestnut.

He walked over to the tall tree, holding the blanket to him like an Indian chief, a strange monk. The ground Klokko tread on was cold and muddy from the thaw. But he felt no chill. Touching the tree's bark, cragged and greenish from years of supporting a variety of other life forms, he was surprised by a softness where he expected something else. It was as if the entire world had shifted on him over the last days, since the strange trip out of his native area, out of his head.

Klokko thought of his mother and the songs she'd sing. How his grandma loved to sing, too. How come when you try to remember the words to such things, all you get is the memory of *all* lullabies. If he were to ever have a kid, he'd sing to him. From now on, he'd only listen to that which came out of his own mouth, his own lungs and memory.

Klokko switched thought patterns. He eyed the woods into which the driver of the car in front of his must have headed. Tried playing his mind like a jukebox, clicking on all the song titles, and actual tunes, he would have mentioned to that old dude Jim if he'd had known what he was talking about. One last rummage before they all got put on a shelf: *Waterloo Sunset* and *Take a Giant Step. It's Only Love* and *Whispering Pines. Wild Horses. In My Room.*

None of them lullabies, or quite as natural as blues tunes. The chickadees' song. His own humming. His breath.

Klokko flashed back on his vinyl LPs. How he liked keeping them out of their sleeves, all rubbing up against each other as if pollinating one another. He used to tell himself that the crackle and snap of the resulting scratches was "Martian Applause." The sound of heaven. Or hell, depending on the mood in which he was thinking such thoughts.

All that music was just cacophony. He stopped, listened. A high wind was moving through the trees, clicking their branches together. When he put his head against the chestnut's tall trunk, he could hear it moan. Like a lullaby. Sounds of patient being. A true chestnut.

Klokko stopped and folded his blanket into the crook of the tree's nearest branch. He'd be back for it. For now, it was a gift.

He found the pool and waterfall he was expecting to find. He'd been here before.

He sank slowly into the cold, relishing the cleanliness of moving water. Sank his beard and graying hair in. Drank, like a dog, from the wetness pouring over him, mouth open to the current. Then rose and shook like a dog. Repeated the cleansing baptism three times, like a ritual.

Klokko thought he heard another whoop. The sort of sound he'd hear Pa make when hitting home after drinking in town.

He clambered out of the pool and sat still until dry, listening. Whatever it was, was gone.

Starting back for the car, Klokko noticed a pile of clothes strewn haphazardly. He walked over for a closer look.

He stood, barefoot, patchy snow around him in the darker recesses of tree-cover and moss, and looked down upon a pair of knit trousers, slightly belled, and a thin, stylish black silk shirt. Some skinny-man-panty underwear sprawled amongst the skinny twig branches of a soon-to-bud tree. Nice, soft socks and a pair of zip up alligator boots on a bed of soggy moss. And in a sagging hemlock: a pair of top-of-the-line sunglasses and a leather suit jacket, tapered at the waist and double-breasted, like he once saw in a magazine while cutting the eyes out of photos.

Klokko thought. I've been good my whole life. I was a proper kid, a decent son. Where has it got me? No love. A pile of songs. Heartache and loneliness. Nothingness.

He reached down and pulled the man-panties on. Snug, a perfect fit. He put on the shirt, the neat trousers. He pulled the socks over his battered feet. It all felt good. Everything fit perfectly, as if tailored just for him.

Dressed like a rock star, Klokko walked to the stream's edge to get a glimpse of his new self in the pool he'd just emerged from. But the water was rippling by too fast to see anything but blur.

"Fuck 'em all," he whispered to himself, turning on his fresh leather heel and sauntering back out of the forest. He'd listened to enough rock and roll. Time for the full-throated roar of a self-possessed attitude.

Klokko thought about his baby blanket but decided he'd lived with the shit thing long enough. Fuck my fucking childhood. I'm my own man. It's all a gift from here on in, anyway. Extra innings.

When he got to his car nothing had changed. He felt in the pocket of his new pants. Keys and some money. A vial of white powder.

He felt himself swagger. He was a changed man. Richie.

Fashion has a way of doing things to men and women, especially in their middle ages.

Klokko eyed the black rent-a-car then walked over to his Delta 88 and peered in at the keys he'd left in the ignition. He shrugged and headed back for the rent-a-car, flipping on the radio as he put it into gear and took off towards Woodstock. He didn't need to coast any more. Hell, this baby had a full tank. Life isn't so bad after all, given the right attitude. Rock and roll as style, and not just a harbor for memory.

A pang of guilt started to flow up his spine. Klokko shook his head and it disappeared. His neck stayed stiff, still.

He turned the radio up.

"It's a sad day here in Woodstock, memorializing one of our chosen sons," came a smooth FM voice. "Folks are flying in from all over for the Memorial Service in Bearsville this evening. Word has it Mr. Dylan, maybe even a Beatle or two, will be there. Yet another sad day for rock and roll...but in its odd way, a catharsis."

Hell's bells, Klokko thought. Could this be what had been pulling him? He thought of all the music he'd heard that morning. The way in which he found himself headed back north towards Woodstock. And how the teenager in the house opposite Sid's Ford, all the silly crushes of his life, had started shedding from him. Like fleas. Like old skin.

He thought of his father, his dreams of reconnecting. He'd find him, his Pa, when the time was right. Now he had another mission. He was finding himself or, at least, learning what it was inside that had been holding him back. Klokko got the sense of what it would be like to have been someone else. What it would be like not to be himself.

"I can write it," he said, interrupting the radio as it talked about the dead man.

Klokko swooped down the mountain past the chapel he'd just attended, past the driveway Stand Back Cato Jim had disappeared into. He put the car into second. More songs played as he descended.

I'm a fucking hypocrite, he thought. I'm a thief.

The smell of burning brakes broke the reverie. He shifted down into first.

He also turned off the radio. Didn't want to be in this dead man's head any longer. He was tired of others' songs, no matter how comfortable they felt, or how good they were at conveying certain moods he'd never have captured, in his past life, without them.

Klokko was pulled. At the bottom of the hill, he took a left at a crossroads surrounded by old farmhouses. He rode with the mountain rising to his left, a new terrain of shale shelves. Piedmont.

Fuck the future, Klokko thought. I *am* rock and roll now. I'm being *me*. I'm a being.

He started to hum. The tune that arose from his lips, lungs, heart, and soul felt original, deep, and resonant.

He took a sharp left onto the first road that appeared, then freed his head of the past once and for all. Succumbed to the beauty of sounds he was making all on his own.

After a mile or so he swung right down a quick cutoff, then took another left. Stoll Road. He knew he was going in the right direction.

The black rent-a-car spun and squealed around sharp corners, descending layer after layer of shale bank cliffs and plateaus. He continued talking aloud.

"Oh Lord, Land-a-Goshen," he shouted. "I'm a roadrunner. I'm a little chickadee!"

He took a sharp right onto Parnassus Drive. Dropped even further as he rode towards what must be a dead-end.

Klokko screeched to a halt just shy of hitting a large, ugly-pink ranch house with a large basement garage door facing him. Shit, he thought. This is my grail?

He turned the car off and sat staring at the place he'd been pulled to. He recognized it, slightly.

No one was around. He got out of the car, stretched. Quietly shut the door and walked up to peer in the garage windows.

Instead of cars and the usual junk, he saw shelves and shelves of vinyl records. LPs, mainly, with only a few boxes of 45s, a few piles of unsleeved 78s, as unkempt as his own Martian Applause.

On the edges of the room were shelves and shelves of 8-tracks. Instruments piled into a corner. A table filled with papers. Altogether, it added up to more music than he'd ever imagined in one place.

Klokko climbed around from the basement and up a steep lawn to the house's front door. Place was nice inside. Much bigger than expected.

"Big Pink?" he thought with a start. Not THE Big Pink?

25

I pass the boarding house's front door and scurry around the edge of the building to where the open window is, careful to remain as unseen as possible for a naked middle-aged dead dude. I want to find out where I've wandered to. Make another call, if possible. Maybe ask for help.

Hell, I just want to catch a glimpse of people and check out their reactions to see whether I *am* dead or not.

Inside an orange-walled, red-ceilinged room sits a tall, bald, Oriental-looking man in a purple robe. He's surrounded by pillows and strange writings reminding me of those guys who called themselves the Bauls of Bengal, Indian dudes who turned everyone in town onto the ways of smoking hash through a chillum. Or those folks from Kurasawa movies. A holy guy, probably Hindu or Buddhist or Zen or something.

The guy's chanting, low. He bangs the gong as I peer, seemingly unnoticed, through the window. I'm stomping foot to foot in the last snow crust. Then all goes silent.

I rap, lightly, at the window.

No response.

Maybe I really am dead. I rap again.

The guy's eyes pop open and he turns my direction, quick as a panther. He stares as I rap against the old window again. He smiles and rises, nodding his head and motioning, with a long, elegant hand, towards the front door I passed.

By the time I get there he has it open, the warmth escaping and pulling me in like a welcoming bath towel held open by one's mother.

"Hey, I hope you don't mind. I think I'm lost and, well…" I blabber as the purple-robed dude shuts the door behind me, clapping his hands together for warmth. He motions me down the hall towards the room he'd just come from.

"Please to follow," he says in a singsong accent. "You're naked. You must want tea? Please. Sit with me. It is your time."

I tell him how I used to live in town but moved away and have been following this kid I thought was my son and I got lost and I went swimming and…I ask him if he thinks I might be dead.

"Of course, you are dead," he replied with a chuckle. "Take tea."

I settle into the silk cushions; he settles down across from me.

"No need for story. You are not lost. You here for good reason," he says when he sees I am comfortable. "No matter that you are ghost. We all go for good reasons. We all stay until then."

When I try to say something else, the monk puts his fingers to his lips and motions to the tea. He takes a sip and savors it, swishing its heat around in his mouth and shutting his eyes as he swallows. He opens his eyes and nods at me. Following his cue, I do the same, savoring the bitter smoky flavor as if it were a Single Malt.

We sit for what seems an eternity. Who knows where the time goes half one's life? Or all one's death, I'm finding out.

I recall that Mason Hoffenberg lived up here, back before I took him in. Last of the Beatniks, everyone called the coot...until he started calling himself by the same nicknames, heavily drinking and drugging himself in the old George Bellows house fast by Rock City Road. Funny dude. He'd co-written *Candy,* the dirty bible.

"Your life just up and becomes a story you don't have the time to read. You think you'll always be successful, but then it starts catching up with you," he said in this long-ass Playboy interview he did while living at my house, telling all my secrets and making me look as bad as him. Which I guess I was. "You wake up one day and see the person, there in the mirror, that you were before the fame. And, so, you try and obliterate him."

It's like Mason entered my soul, with everything he said becoming what I say now. My death his death. Before or after, would it matter?

The monk again sounds his gong and I shake my head.

"You see now?" he asks, refilling my cup. "It's a crazy story, life, and death. You know about forgiveness? Forget sin, it's forgiveness that matters."

When he takes another sip, closing his eyes, I take my cue. As the warm liquid descends my throat my mind takes off once more. This time I slip into a familiar-looking kitchen with a wood stove, the leftovers of a Thanksgiving feast on the table. Sort of like that first holiday in town at Happy and Jane's place when we were all just starting to grow beards and try our own sound, still amazed at the wonders of life off the road. Money not a worry and a town all ours for hanging in.

Something's off, though. The music that's playing is coming out of one of those newfangled CD thingies. The wine labels read late 1990s. I hear crying and step into another room and realize it's not

Thanksgiving but some other party that's gone on too long. People are grieving.

"His heart just gave out, the big lunk," Rick's wife is saying between sobs. She's older. Lizzie, graying and sad-eyed, has her arm around her. Strange how you recognize faces from your past beyond the aging.

So, my bandmate and running partner Rick's died, too. It feels like my diaphragm's just dropped, like all the wind's left me.

"All dying," Lizzie says.

I open my eyes. The monk is smoking a cigarette. He motions for me to sip more tea.

"You said something about your son," he says. "You have to see your father."

And there he is, Ed, my Pa, rough, oil-stained hands on the kitchen table after his own pa, my grandad, passed away. Ma kneading his thick neck muscles. My brothers all sitting there as I come in from band practice, hair stiffened into a pompadour for the first time.

Everything goes quiet in the cabbage-smelling room as the old man stands before me. I try passing him by, heading for the basement I'd moved into. Sour mash breath in my face.

"Have you no blasted decency about you, boy. This is a time for mourning."

I do my loosey-goosey thing and wham! He smacks me upside the new do. And that's him for me.

"Get yourself a trade, Richie," he says, as I rub my ear, grinning like he'd just eaten a cat. "Give this music thing up and get growed. Make something of yourself."

Now I'm at the same table with my brothers, all older. No Ma hovering over the stove.

"First Pa, then Richie," Bobby says. "Now Ma..."

The scene feels black and white, like a foreign film needing titles.

"I should have spent time with him," I say.

The monk is looking at me with a kind, knowing smile, my mother's look of understanding in his eyes. He takes the empty cup from my hand and rises, motioning for me to rise, too. He walks me to the door.

"Follow the road. A car awaits you" he says in his gentle singsong. "Through the trees, 500 steps."

I want to ask him what this death thing means.

"We grow as we grow," he says. "The biggest stories move very slowly, generation to generation."

He opens the door to a blast of cold air.

"You go free now," he says, making a little bow, his hands together in prayer formation. "Forgive the father. Forgive yourself."

I start to say something but the monk smiles and places his finger to his lips. The door shuts.

I turn. The forest I'd come out of is lit with mid-afternoon sun. I count my steps, listening for the water, remembering my nakedness.

I think I hear it in the distance. Also, some whooping sound, like an echo of my own recent hollering. I walk faster until I see the glinting reflection of my car.

But no clothes. I look around. What about my car keys?

I breathe in, breathe out. It is going to be okay.

I figure my sense of time's gone nutso. Or I'm out of time.

There's a blanket in an old tree's crook. Baby blue with sailboats, like something from my own past. I wrap myself in it.

All I find back at the road is a rusty shit-green Oldsmobile Delta 88 where my nifty black rent-a-car had been.

I peer in the car's window. At least there are keys in the ignition. Should I?

I think of the monk's goofy grin. Didn't he say there's always a need for slapstick, some comedy of errors, a bit of wabi-sabi, upside-down clickety-clack? Or something of that sort?

I get in the car, start the thing up. The engine coughs, red fuel light on. I try the radio, fiddle with the dial. Woodstock again. My songs. My death.

I hit a button and the thing whirs to a more commercial station from down the valley.

Some hit about not being forgotten.

It feels good to feel the old car's cloth seat under my naked ass. Its boat-like movement.

I wrap the baby blanket around my dead self.

26

Klokko squeezed in behind some razor bushes and cupped his hands to Big Pink's windows. The furniture was basic Montgomery Ward: a two-part sectional sofa set facing a glass-fronted wood stove. A Bentley rocker and shellacked raw wood slab coffee table piled high with coffee table books, the new *A Day in the Life of America* on top. A big glass ashtray, emptied and clean. A television on a rolling set-up.

Under the room's long windows, catty-corner to where Klokko peered in, was a birch and glass cabinet filled with books. Under the window across from him was a similar piece topped with a combined turntable and cassette player unit. Shelves were filled with records.

An infant bouncy seat dangled from molding over the entrance to the kitchen/dining half of the big room. One of those rolling circular baby tables that you put a screaming kid into. A basket of teething toys and soft blocks over by the bookcase.

Klokko imagined what the place must have looked like back when Richard Manuel and the rest of his band lived and worked in this place. All he'd seen, over the years on album covers, was the basement filled with instruments, sound baffles, recording equipment, beer cans, ashtrays. What he imagined was the antithesis of the Big Pink he was peering into.

He thought of his own abode: the red boiler room, his grandparents' former boarding house and farm falling in around him. Things stuck wherever they'd been placed. Stuff piled up.

It was oh so different when Ma was well. Before her illness—for all his life up until he turned 30—Ma'd kept a neat home. Handed-down Duncan Phyfe, wingback chairs, a camelback sofa, oval rag-stitch area rugs. Knickknacks on hand-stitched doilies; framed illustrations on the walls. A few paint-by-numbers finished before Pa cut off such fun as being too frivolous.

Klokko's family had a television for a couple of weeks. Gerard kept a phonograph in his room, later passed down to Klokko. Lost to the barn collapse. The brothers kept records under the bed like Ma kept books and magazines in her sewing closet.

For as long as Klokko could remember, Pa couldn't abide entertainment. Except for the newspaper he'd read at the end of day, its funny pages growing grimily unreadable as he wiped his mechanic's hands on them, shuffling between news and sports.

Klokko's mother had once told him, when she was in hospital, that Pa's hatred of entertainment and all "artsy fartsy" things was the result of a job he'd held as a kid down at the Catskills' only Ford dealership. His own childhood and heartbreak.

Knowing Mt. Calvary inside out for the 13 years he'd lived there, first in the barn and then in the boiler room, Klokko could fully understand. But that didn't quell the hurt. The mystery he'd been swamped by ever since his Pa disappeared after Ma's death. The man had never talked about likes and dislikes, about emotions or anger. He never said anything. What Klokko knew of Mt. Calvary he'd learned from being there or remembered from the stories Ma started telling him as she died.

She and his father had met, she told him, when she was working in Utica as a school secretary. Having grown up in a small town near the Vermont border, she'd started out at Junior College in Troy aiming for a teacher's degree, but then settled on something more practical when her dad's business took a turn for the worse.

But that was nothing compared to the hardships Klokko's Pa had come through. The family farm on Mt. Calvary started failing before the New Deal, before Black Friday. Ed, Klokko's Pa, got work as a car mechanic's errand boy before he turned ten.

When the war came, he signed up fast. Met Gladys, Klokko's Ma, while off base one night from Pine Camp. They married before he shipped out. Had Gerard while he was island-hopping in the Pacific, losing new buddies, then spawned Klokko when home for his ma's funeral.

Klokko's dad had been an only child. After he buried his parents, he shut up the farm, forgot about it except for the few times he'd take the family up there for a picnic at Gladys's urging.

He moved Klokko's Ma to Pine Camp, which became Fort Drum, which is where both Gerard and he were born. Pa took to the older boy as if he were a gift sent to salve the wounds caused by his mother's passing, the war. The second son, Richie, was treated like a vivid reminder of death's omnipresent shadow over life.

Once, when Klokko asked why Pa had buried his grandparents the way he did, Ma answered by saying that, given the way they'd gone, it only seemed right.

Crows sounded behind Klokko, dressed in his rock and roll gear.

He'd always wanted his father to love him, to pick him up and hug him. Or later, in high school when he found himself so shy, so pained. Or after Gerard died. And Ma.

He'd wanted his father to forgive and love himself.

"I forgive you, Pa. I accepted what I could. You didn't," Klokko said through the glass to the empty room in Big Pink. "I forgive you, Pa, for pushing Gerard to wildness where you had none. Not his fault. Not yours."

Klokko forgave his brother for dying, forgave his Ma for growing ill and not being able to defeat the cancer that got her. Things happen. Death has no dominion. And neither do we.

"I forgive myself, Lord," he said, hands on the Big Pink's glass.

Klokko realized how we become obsessed with our pain, which consumes us. Makes us hate everything that isn't hurtful. It makes you need to disappear.

The room seemed to speak back to Klokko. Entertainment was an excuse. Like everything created in this pink house's basement. A shill treated as art.

Klokko stepped away from the window. His new-found confidence rocked against waves of newly uncovered disappointments. He stepped back through the razor bushes, making sure not to rip his new duds.

He shook his head. Cleared his throat. Started to belt out a song that rose from within him.

"Standing by this window..." came the words.

He paused to catch his breath for a second line.

27

I turn the radio off. I'm in a good mood. I coast down this mountain in second, then first, the better to save the brakes. It's a lesson I learned through experience. Don't ask.

I nod in the direction of Father Francis' little Church on the Mount, half-hidden in forest. Dylan used to say how he got many of his treasured words from the old priest's way of passing on bible stories, perfect quotes for whatever occasion people wanted him to get a handle on.

Ah, our mental jukeboxes. I settle on that guy Guitar's cocka-mamie idea about getting us aging rock and rollers to do oldies acts for the masses. For him. As if we could all be living jukeboxes like the Beach Boys became after Brian went off the deep end. Would *he* ever make it back?

No matter how dry my creative juices become, I have to main-tain some pride. That's why I'm here in Woodstock. Why we all returned, except for Robbie.

I figure that no matter how empty this Oldsmobile's tank might get, or how dead I stay or don't stay, I'll get to where I need to go. I'll somehow end up somewhere beyond where I am. No limbo for this boy, even if I'm in some shit dream, some vomitous hallucination of a fucked-up cat's dream tied back to that asshole-on-the-mountain's shitty-ass drugs.

The car keeps rolling slow as I shift into neutral. My hands stay on the wheel as it moves towards where it plans to give up the ghost and choke out its last gasps for gas. I just need a couple more stops.

What do we think of people when they fade from our day-to-day reality? It's one thing to be on the radio, another to be buried in someone's record collection. Eventually, everything gets shuffled. We move beyond music.

Will I become this unnamable force of nature that'll force my exes, my old bandmates, my kid, into years of therapy? Regret? Will Junior end up fitting me into this little box filled with bogeymen and monsters, similar to where I pushed the memories of my own father, passed away long after I'd already buried him via the drink, the drugs, the sex, the fucking rock and roll that had sunk my own fatherhood and doomed me to this present meaningless narrative, drawn forward by forces I can't seem to affect?

Oh father, please, please forgive me. I'm sorry. And I now forgive you. Really.

Houses pop into view as the outskirts of my old hometown rise around me. They're fancier than what I've been seeing throughout the rest of Upstate. Recent paint jobs. Fixed-up porches with real porch furniture. Manicured flower beds instead of the ticky-tack, bent-over-gardener sculpture and chainsaw carvings that pass for culture in too many places. Woodstocky, I guess they call it. Wood trellises and annual garden tours you pay good money to get on, gawking at everyone's knack for the 'horty culture.'

The high, wispy clouds and wide vistas remind me of back roads I'd ride in Ontario as a kid. And that, in turn, reminds me of my Ma and Pa's front porch, the smell of Spring stretching up from the lakes to beckon us out onto the street for stickball and soccer. Girls. Liquor. Drugs. As a kid, I liked nothing better than running through woods. Then standing still under an open sky. That sense of being on the edge of something being spun in the reflection of a bigger light. Like an epiphany, I guess.

Or maybe just a bug about to hit a sky-reflecting windshield.

I'm looking forward to getting back to town and being around folks, talking to someone other than myself. Proving my non-death.

I'm a changed man now.

I think how the rock and rollers playing bars are all old now. I haven't seen any seventeen-year-olds playing in ages. If Junior were to follow in my steps, he could make something of himself. Wasn't Lennon's forgotten kid doing that, with a top-twenty hit riding the radio waves for the past year or so? And that rastaman Marley's boy? Before you knew it, there'd be Dylans, and Mitchells, and Youngs, and McCartneys ruling the airwaves, directing all the movies, designing clothes, and running for the same political offices their moms and dads had secretly wished they could have held.

I come down to the crossroads where I can either head straight to the green, off to the right in the direction of Bearsville, or scoot back out of town to the left.

I sense, rather than see or hear, something large flutter by. There's a thud on the roof. An owl's face bends down, its dark-rimmed unblinking eyes staring into mine.

This can't be real. Another owl swoops across the road, the face before me disappears. I watch as the second white owl follows the first to my left.

Guess that's where I'll be going.

I make the turn, shift up, add a spurt of gas, and coast a bit more, the escarpment of high mountains rising above the empty passenger's side of this strange old car. I just might make it, I think. I'm just not sure to where.

I look down at my skinny nakedness half wrapped in another's blanket. No wonder I'm dead. I wasted away. Too many drugs. Too little care for the art of living. I'm covered in cuts and scrapes, bruises, and abrasions.

I slow down, passing the house where I believe Lizzie and Junior are living. I eye the driveway for a car. Thankfully, I don't see any. I'm not ready to see what they say about my present dilemma, naked as the day I was born, headed for judgment. Unsure whether I'm dead or alive.

I let the car pull me on with its last fumes of fuel. Left onto West Saugerties Road, then right onto Goat Hill, left again onto Stoll Road. I'd coasted this before. Many times.

Maybe I was dead before. Which means I can be alive, still.

I want to visit Big Pink, our legendary house of basement creativity. It holds good memories. Maybe a clue, too, as to what I'm doing on this strange trip. Maybe there *is* a second chance. The boys could be there. Liz. Dawn. It'd be like a surprise party, with my old writing chops as a present. Bob smiling my direction from the upright piano, sliding over on the bench just enough to make some room for me. Robbie laughing, not all tight-ass about schedules or contracts. We can start over, doing everything right this time. I'll buy the house and rebuild our lives there, writing about family and friendship, spirit, and worldly hope and not just the self-pity and sorrow of a twenty-year-old's yearning.

I hit Parnassus Drive with just enough in this old car to run the slight rise before the tank burps its last and I coast down a last dip. The engine dies and I roll on in.

The big pink house sits just as I remember her. And you know what? So does my rent-a-car.

God sure works in the strangest ways. I must be rising, no matter how slowly, to heaven now. Land-a-Goshen. I must be beyond the worst.

I stop, wait, and watch. I soak in the quiet.

Then I see this guy. Edge of my vision. Has my clothes on. Looks like me but as seen through some strange mirror.

This death-like vision of life; could I be seeing a vision of my kid as me, all grown into a man?

I open the door of the car quietly as the man peers into a window and catches my reflection. He startles, stiff like a deer, then takes off as I swing out the car and follow him towards the woods.

"Man, I just have some questions. Man!?!" I yell, running.

The two of us scamper through hemlocks. It's like I'm floating above the forest floor. I don't feel the sticks and stones, the wet leaves and remaining cold of snow and ice on my bare feet. Just a will to connect with this running dude in my clothes.

I stop in a spot under an old maple, gouged, and twice the size of everything around me. I used to sit here.

"Hey, mister," I yell out as I see the mirror-me cut back into Big Pink's yard, the escarpment of the mountain known as Overlook rising high behind us. He's headed for an old bicycle leaned up against the basement wall. An old bicycle. Looks the same as one I used to ride, 20 years earlier.

The man stops and looks back in my direction, blank-faced. Then he nods his head, gets on the bike, and heads off up the driveway past both our cars.

Holy fuck, I think. The monk was right. This is slapstick.

I take off across the lawn. The afternoon sky's starting to deepen, show some orange. It's drop-dead beautiful.

I see that the doppelganger's gone and left MY keys in MY rent-a car. It takes a moment to maneuver out from behind what must be his Delta 88. I turn off the radio with its ongoing symphony of me. I know where to look. I tear out the driveway like I used to, bottoming out as I go.

Hitting Goat Road, I see the dude head down West Saugerties Road on his bike. This is going to be a snap, I figure. I turn the radio back on and slow the car, watching the guy on the bike peddling furiously ahead of me. Some song asks us both to relax. Comedy of errors, most definitely.

I flash on the City's new club scene; the massive Palladium, where we once played New Year's when it was still the Academy. Area and its living dioramas. Creepy. Privates and its music videos, the giant theme restaurant called America. Downtown Beirut, for God's sake, over on the edge of Alphabet City.

"Relax Relax Relax," I hear as I ease behind the peddler, worrying for a split second that he might shoot off over the trees like ET.

The song ends abruptly and, sure as shit, the bike and its rider shoot down a driveway I never noticed before. I hit the brakes, start backing up, and turn into where he's just gone. He re-enters the road I was on another hundred yards down. I turn the radio off and back out to the main road.

One thing about having spent so much time learning to be the lovable town drunk is that you learn that town inside out.

I'm drawn by this version of myself I'm chasing, as if my dreams had shifted to real and vice versa. You know how it is? Finish, then open your eyes. Don't piss yourself.

I pull over, check my dead self out in the rearview. Not bad. Moving it around I check out what parts of my body I can get into view. Not bad, either. At least there's no light shining through.

After a few minutes, I figure the guy in my clothes has enough head start and I hit the gas, hurtling down West Saugerties until I bank fast onto Glasco, Steve McQueening into town.

I screech down Plochmann, racing past Lee's barn, where I holed up with Dawn the previous year. No time for niceties now. I look down side streets, amongst newer modulars for the bicyclist. Emptiness. Not even stray pets or parked cars.

The town looks comforting this way. Homey. Just as me in my nakedness feels alright, now. Without the pain of self-consciousness or physical discomforts. No druggy haze. No need for humility, let alone grief and the agony of finally being let loose into the great wherever I've spent half my life dreading and trying to get away from.

Okay. I *am* dead.

I stop at Plochmann's intersection with 212 in town and decide there's really no need for me to be chasing. It's a small town, instinctively incestuous. I'll catch up with him soon enough, either at my own funeral or some other such strange occasion.

With time to kill, I take a right and start to make my way up Mill Hill Road and Tinker Street towards Bearsville. Given I'm gone, there must be some sort of service for me. And those things tend to start at sundown, which we're about an hour away from. It'll be at the theater, Albert's unfinished place.

If I am dead, I've got some things to gather before I lose these moments of clarity. If I've been drawn back for my own fucking funeral, there must be some good left of me. Someone's got to have a plan.

What used to be the A&P shines as always, but with fewer cars out front. A pile of soot at one end of the parking lot tells me it was a harsh February. The convenience store's windows are as steamed up as my motel room a few days earlier. Better beware, I think. The Village Green's looking scraggly, muddier than lawn-like. Some kids are seated on a bench. Some old hippie sorts, new to me, beating on drums. Rocky, jittering as usual. But no one's waving or making faces. Could my death have fucked this place up this bad?

Folks are walking in the same direction I'm heading, the sky going red above us. They're bundled up, hands to their necks, eyes down or blankly looking ahead, as if the temperature had dropped twenty. No one notices my black car passing, or me in it, naked. Looking out with what must have been the only smile left in town that hour.

Naked like this...I figure it wouldn't be good form to stop by the library to see if Lizzie's there.

I notice, for memory's sake, that most of the cop cars are out from the lot behind Town Hall. Too bad; I had wanted to give THEM a wave. Talk about the best possible way to check how real I might be.

I figure it best to forego driving into the parking lot of my own memorial. I take a left and head up to the Comeau, where the town offices are, the soccer fields dotted with dog shit. Another good spot to walk when one felt like walking.

Which I do, just now.

I pull into an empty lot up there and scamper across the parking lot into playing fields, aimed for the woods.

In a flash, I've descended into trees, everything cast in a reddish-purple hue by the setting sun.

28

A car rolled silently into the driveway thirty feet from Klokko, stopping his first attempt at full-throated singing since he was a kid.

It was not just any car, but *his* old green Oldsmobile. A naked man was driving. Bearded. Graying. Angry-eyed. Same dude who had been at Sid's Ford, talking to his Lady. A man like himself.

Klokko darted up the lawn, not about to try for a getaway in the car he'd stolen from this guy staring him down.

He started running into the forest then stopped, recalling a bicycle back by the basement doors. He'd take that.

He ran back towards the house and passed within ten feet of the naked man, covered in his baby blanket with the sail-boats, hollering at the top of his lungs as he reached and then ran-started his ride on a girl's Raleigh. He took off up the driveway, wobbling because it had been a couple of decades since he'd been on two-wheeled transportation of any kind. He headed for the road to Woodstock he'd just come down from.

Even though he knew his pursuer would be soon coming out of the Big Pink driveway in the black rent-a-car, all the fear started seeping out of Klokko. The naked, bearded guy wasn't after him, but somehow after the same mysterious thing he was after. He glanced over his shoulder and saw him not looking his way at all. The guy was staring at Big Pink. Just as he had.

He had heard the man call out to him, saying there was no need to run.

Klokko listened intently to the ensuing silence punctuated by his pedaling, his breath. He checked out the woods rising on either side of the road he was on.

He could have been a good father, given the opportunities. Change *could* occur, he thought. Things *can* still happen. I *can* run. I can move on *my* own terms, of *my* own accord. Maybe even make a family, finally. Get a job.

Acceptance is a plot twist, an action, as strong as any heroic dive into the unknown, Klokko figured. It's just quieter, harder to tell tales about.

He hit an incline and stood on the pedals to get more speed. Looking over his shoulder, Klokko again looked for the car he'd just been driving. He noted the play of March light against the rock faces above him. Saw that first tinge of pink and purple in the tree branches that augured the coming of Spring.

Should he stop for his pursuer?

His new boots, oddly comfortable, seemed to pump the bike's pedals of their own accord. He seemed to already be in contact with this man behind him, as if in a dream. Something big was pulling the two of them down towards the valley, towards that mythical rock and roll town he'd long heard about but never visited.

"That's Overlook," he said, aloud, motioning his head to the mountain which dominated to his right. He careened into a nearby driveway and cut across a lawn to a second driveway, then a third, as he spotted the black car speed by through the woods, the naked man's head turning back and forth looking. The man pulled in across the way, did a three-point turn, and headed back towards Big Pink.

Klokko took the opportunity and shot back out onto the main road and took off.

Before long, the side road Klokko was on teed into a larger roadway with a double yellow line down its middle. Heavier traffic, but he didn't mind for once. He wasn't naked. He had cool clothes. He was wearing shades. People might even think he was someone other than who he was. And he was surprisingly fast, headed downhill now.

This time, it would be the naked pursuer who would have to hide. Not Klokko. He, Richie, would just have to keep on moving on.

He turned off into more driveways and yards, then somehow ended up riding into a series of flat forest trails.

Woodstock seemed a mixture of New England village and wealthy suburb. White houses with painted trim. Stone walls. A rough, forested terrain mixed with nice lawns. Cultivated mountain ruggedness. It didn't feel quite right.

No one was around. No dogs barked. The cars whirred by up the hill on the road he'd been on.

Klokko emerged out of a forested path into the potted parking lot behind a shopping center. He thought about stopping and peering in an open trash container but decided it best to keep moving. He wasn't really that hungry; just old habits haunting him in his new skin. He was part of a team's action now. He and the dude in his blanket.

He pedaled around the shopping plaza and onto the town's main thoroughfare, a slight hill of a street lined with gas stations, a grocery store, tall bare trees. He noticed ragged, hippie types every-where, mingled in with tie-dyed tourists as he slowed his pedaling.

Klokko passed a grassy triangle in front of a church. Several people beating on drums, repeating that same dirge-like sound he'd heard those New Hope kids, Harry and Santa, playing by the river.

He looked behind him for the naked follower. The man was gone. But still following, he figured. He knew what it was to be naked in a car. You had to do it careful. Like the naked man must be doing now.

He looked up into the sky and figured it must be nearing sunset. Colors emerging, deepening. He rode past a bookstore, a wine shop, some place selling tacos. People nodded at Klokko as he passed, as if they knew who he was. Or should have known. The sun arced away.

"Excuse me," Klokko stopped a large, pony-tailed man with a shriveled hand seated on a bench across from the drummers. "Would you be able to tell me where the service is?"

"Sure can, pardner," replied the big man. "Just straight out that way a couple miles. You playing or praying?"

Klokko smiled, glad his borrowed shades hid the darting look in his eyes as he thought of an answer.

"Everyone's coming in, you know. Old-time week in town. Just like old hippies to mourn their own," the man continued. "You look familiar. You used to live around here?"

"Not really," was all Klokko could reply. "Gotta go."

Taking off, he heard the man with the strange hand yell after him.

"You're not planning on riding all the way out there and back, are ya?" he bellowed, turning heads up and down the main street. "Shuttle bus starts running in half an hour."

Klokko darted back into an alley that led to a parking lot. He spotted a glimmering behind trees and coasted down to a creek. Followed a road alongside it until a dirt path ran back uphill. Rode up and into a darkening forest lit, intermittently, by swaths of hazy, green-tinged light.

He stashed the bike in a copse of holly and started to walk silently, as he'd learned to do when a boy. Feel for the softness of moss, needle cover. Careful not to snap a twig.

Klokko was used to moving through life pulled by the roles he'd learned to play as a kid. Later, when he found what he liked to think of as *his* own soundtrack, he simply kept at the same games, albeit in new guises. Scared kid/peacock rocker. Fortunate son/jilted lover. Under all thumbs/*Jumping Jack Flash*. Mystic-bound threshold-dweller with a Knowledge Book, boy trapped in blue silk up in the evil king's tower.

This was different.

Klokko hunkered down *Combat*-style and moved over spongy swamps of half-melted ice-edged snow and frost blocks of dirt and branches. Kept arms close to his sides. Looked for paths.

The naked man at Big Pink had spooked him. It was like a version of himself from before the forest pool, like the self-image he'd seen over time in windows, his rearview, his mind's eye. Had his soul split in two?

The man might be a kindred spirit, though. Weren't these lands filled with such?

In a clearing were two fawns and a doe. Klokko stood silent, watching. He'd seen this scene before. Twice. Once as a kid. He'd told Gerard about it, who'd told him to tell Ma as she lay sick in bed with one of her headaches. It had made her smile. The other time was with Pa, after the deaths. Father had a gun, drunk, and was telling him he had to learn how to be a man. Whacked him one when he dropped the gun Pa passed to him, knowing he couldn't possibly shoot the fawns. It would have been like shooting himself, what was left of his good memories, his hope. Then Pa shot the doe.

"No need to worry," said an older female voice with a British accent. "They're used to people. Can't really feed themselves anymore. They take no care about human voices, human cars."

A reddish-gray-haired woman was seated on a tripod stool behind a paint-splattered wood easel. On it was a portrait of a bearded man in sunglasses, two-thirds finished. The face seemed familiar.

"Looks like you, doesn't it?" the woman said. "You headed for the service?"

Klokko nodded.

"It starts in about an hour. I'll be missing it. Enough death already. I'll paint the man's portrait out here. See if I can put him back in nature where he belongs. He meant a great deal to this town, to our times."

She lifted a hand and pointed in the direction he had been headed.

"Just down there," she said. "Follow the field as it dips to the road. That'll be Sled Hill. Then straight on a mile or so. Past Russell's Pool. You can't miss it."

Klokko noticed that while she talked, her painting hand was deftly adding in leaves and wildflowers, fast and nimble.

"First, take this apple to the doe," she added, handing him a half-eaten Golden Delicious. "It's a ritual."

Klokko looked over his shoulder, wanting to see the naked man. What had happened to him?

"There's a man following me. Like me, but naked," he said to the old painter. "Can we give the apple to him, instead?"

In the clearing the three deer looked expectantly towards him and the painter lady.

"Remember the ritual," the woman replied. "The ritual always rules."

There were others walking along the road when he got to it. People parking their cars wherever they could find a place. Klokko thought the whole happening quite strange, more like a festival than a memorial service, funeral, or whatever it is one calls such things.

He remembered when they buried Gerard, his beloved brother. That was at the funeral home in town. Casket closed. No tears, just Pa, drunk and talking nervously the whole time. And Klokko, holding up Ma.

Up ahead was a carved wooden sign with a bear on it; a policeman directing traffic. Several large buildings in various barn-like shapes, painted red with green trim like some upscale version of classic New England country. He slipped through a thin hedge of soon-to-blossom forsythia to avoid meeting the cop.

With Ma, the casket was open, Klokko remembered as he pushed aside branches and emerged into a fallow field filled with parked cars. He recalled how waxen she looked. Not quite real. She was cold when he touched her. The skin was like wax.

Klokko made his way around the crowd gathering in the brand-new gravel parking lot by going through a copse of tall hemlocks, not unlike those surrounding the chilly pool where he'd found the clothes he was now wearing. In the midst of it was a small clearing of grass and three stones.

He walked up to the big barn with windows overlooking the grass, the stream. The red of the setting sun blared against the vast expanses of glass. Inside, he knew, people would be too busy looking at each other to glance outside where he wandered, apart from the scene he'd never been part of, but felt oddly drawn towards.

Klokko walked up to a picture window and peered in. People in all manner of dress were looking through yet another picture window to someplace deeper within from whence music was coming. It sounded like that version of *I Shall Be Released* he'd heard in Philadelphia. The voices were many. He added his to the mass.

As Klokko peered into the room, one face looked in his direction. He thought it might be his own reflection, in glass, way across the room where there was another window. But as everyone in between him and his reflection looked away, many with tears streaming their faces, he noticed that the window he was seeing was not like the one he was looking through. This was no reflection, he thought. And that man had no clothes on.

He pulled back fast, as though caught at something he couldn't abide.

When he looked again, the face was gone.

Klokko took off running before he knew what had taken hold of him.

It was the naked man, again. It looked like his father. But worse, it looked even more familiar, the way that death's image in the rear-view can, when we see not only our parents but our own skulls glaring sadly as we rocket into a blurring future.

The naked man was Klokko. Klokko was Richie. It was all him. Me.

29

The forest feels like a fur coat, warm and inviting.

I follow the shrinking light until I stumble across a clearing. A voice assails me.

"Right on time, Richard," I hear a lilting British accent say.

I turn and see an older lady with long orange tresses, flecked in gray. She's barely visible in the shadow of the trees, standing before an easel on which sits what looks like a portrait of me captured for eternity right here in this glen, all flower-shrouded like an Ophelia or something. And everybody thinking me the Hamlet!

Before I can express what astonishment's left in me, which is little, she hands me a half-eaten apple. When I go to tell her something she puts a finger to her lips and motions me, with her eyes, towards a beautiful sight: Two fawns and a doe in the glade before us, caught by a shaft of what appears to be dark blue light.

"Don't be late," I think I hear the lady say as I stand still, the deer approaching. They stand and stare a long moment before I realize the sun's set, the woods are now dark, and the woman, her easel and her painting are all vanished. I hold the apple for the doe. She shakes her head my direction. The deer scurry.

It hits me, what I need to do to make this story once more my own. Like it had been when I was a kid. When I first learned to play the piano, the drums, my own vocal cords. Like it was scoring girls in junior high. And then Lizzie. Like it was making those first records. Writing my songs, singing them. Having a kid. Accepting my father's passing. And now dead, myself. Yet coming back here, like this.

I've had my times. Now comes the heroic part...if I can manage it.

I need to remember, bodily, what it felt like to have a little chest breathing in and out warmly against my own naked chest. And what it felt like to be that little chest, letting out my first cries, that first sad song, on my own daddy's body.

Wipe tears away. Smile. Laugh. Remember to walk.

I get to thinking how it was stumbling towards marriage. That moment when love leaped from the sought-for or avoided and into the real. The leap from escaping one's birth family to creating one's own. Leaving oneself a parent as well as a child.

I reach down and run the back of my hand across the wet moss and chill loamy earth on the forest floor and, head lower than it has been for hours, see through the canopy to the lights of Tinker Street not a hundred yards away.

There's a steady stream of cars heading west.

A lifetime's shirking has done no good. All the responsibility I've turned away from lands solidly, albeit pleasantly, on my shoulders. I rise and start to walk towards the moving light, edging out of the woods onto Sled Hill.

I want to tell Liz how much I appreciated her love all these years. And still treasure it. I feel ready, finally, to say the same to Dawn, to Joe and the fellas. Robbie. Bob.

I want to tell my boy I would always love HIM.

The plan I hatched, high up there in the St. Moritz with the Lizard King, was quite simple. I called Liz and told her I had to go to this wedding outside Toronto, where she was living. I actually searched one out by getting an old high school friend to call a few small-town Ontario papers until they found something suitable. Never saw those people before or since. I just hope, now, that their lives turned out okay.

I picked Lizzie up and went on and on about how much I'd been hearing about her modeling career, and how well our band was starting to do. She said she'd heard about me, too. I told her I'd heard she'd been engaged but broke it off. We laughed a lot and I said the wedding we were headed to was for some long-lost relative. I'd promised my family I'd attend. Some awkward dude nicknamed Clocky-o or some such silliness, short for some longer Slavic something-or-other.

We drove across the Ontario flats into lake country. And I just up and proposed to her in a whisper as soon as that unknown groom went and kissed that unknown bride. Then took her off to this cabin in the woods and, well...that was the first time I actually sang *You Don't Know Me* to anyone besides myself. Along with every other song I knew.

Everyone is milling around at the service when I arrive. I move in the shadows, tree to tree, as people head in from the bar area to take their seats. I remember a back door to the old barn, on the café side where we'd stumble out at dawn, all sped out from our Go Fasters. It was sheltered by tall trees. It might just be open. I could get a glimpse of what was happening around, over, and after me.

But it's shut.

I head to the creekside glass windows of the bar area. I get up on tippy toes and try to look in, still holding on to the blue-boated baby blanket I'd found.

People hug each other; they're doing as we're supposed to do in such situations. Everyone looks grieved. Same thing on a few television monitors that are broadcasting live from the main theater, where musicians have gathered.

I see Liz looking radiant with tear-streaked cheeks. She's wearing the little black dress I remember her in from that first night on Yonge Street.

With her, looking like me at his age, is Junior, all chicken neck and black corduroy blazer, skinny tie, jeans. No emotion on his face…a chip off my old block. Thank heavens he hadn't figured out that drunk is the only form of grief for many men. They're holding hands and talking with Happy and his wife, who say something in the boy's direction. At which he breaks composure and grins ear to ear. Goofy-like, you could say.

In another part of the room, I see Dawn all alone. Rick heads her way, puts a big bear-like arm around her as she buries her head in his shoulder. Then his wife comes up and hugs them both. Garth is sitting on a bench all alone, looking like he's fast asleep, while Levon has a bevy of folks around him, laughing.

I scan the crowd for the guys I want most to see…Robbie and Bob. My old buddy Van. Unless they've already entered the theater and are already up on stage, they're not here. And from the sedate, un-frazzled, and down-home feel of the crowd, I'd have to surmise they *haven't* showed, and sent word that they wouldn't be coming.

At least Rick'll be able to pick up where I left off. He could always sing my old songs...better than me in recent years, if anyone would have spoken the truth around me.

Is this what it always comes down to, that deep hidden wonder we have about how people will miss us after we've gone?

I'm a naked dead man on the verge of tears, staring through cold glass at those who've gathered to sum up my sad life.

But I catch myself. I am yet a man. Someone with a plan, however odd and sepulchral. I just need to find my opening amidst all the glittery ball of confusion that's part and parcel with viewing one's own funeral. Will it be hard reaching out of this final dream, breaking whatever watery wall is still between me and whatever it takes to make a real difference in others' lives...a difference that's cogent, useful, and not just perceived after the fact as ironic?

I am dead but I am returning!

Concentrate, man, I tell myself. Get your kid's attention without scaring everyone else who's here for you. Don't make a scene. Rip into the canvas, break the fourth wall. Write that bridge, the hook that'll capture all those stray emotions everyone's looking to find a song for. Save the kid! Be a dad, a real father, and not just a man whose sperm got loose.

I notice old school buds, band members from my teens. Ma and my brothers must be doing something else back home. Do I need to go there, too? I don't think so. One trip's enough for what needs to be done.

Everybody has their eyes on the door, looking for bigger names. Same with me.

Someone inside the theater, beyond what I can see across the still-crowded barroom with its plexiglass window, is on the stage talking. People turn towards the television monitors, crowd around them so I can't tell what's what. I want to walk right in there, naked as the day I was born, and throw my arms out and bellow some song for everyone. Or at least ask that they include me in the proceedings, let me get a glimpse of the tube.

Junior seems to be the only person refusing to go into the main room, despite his mother's entreaties from the door. Good...I must be pulling at his consciousness. Just look over this way, boy, and I will change your future. "This way, Junior," I whisper. "We'll change all our futures."

Something catches my eye across the room, through the picture windows and the double-paned windows beyond that. I look away from my son and he's gone, disappeared with his mother into the room where they're celebrating my damned death.

I seem to be looking straight at Junior as an older man, staring through the window of time back at me. But no, it's that dude who stole my clothes and rent-a-car.

The truth hits me. I AM gone.

The man I'm seeing is as dead as me. He IS me, gazing from the other side.

We both start away from the windows, and I stumble painfully, nakedly, off the embankment and down a tangle of icy moss and branches into the middle of the creek.

In the stream stands the old guy who'd met me at my door in Winter Park. Cato, with the Stand Back baseball cap still on his head, haloed by the spillover lights of the service's windows. Grinning, no less.

"You shouldn't be running anymore," he says. "You've al-most climbed that mountain, son. Wouldst thou follow me the remainder of the way, please?"

I seem to rise out of my battered body to watch myself scamper up the stream into darkness.

"Never mind the other half," the old man continues. "We'll catch up with him and bring him forth."

He stops and turns. Takes my hand and leads me up the ice-edged stream to where it meets a wider waterway. We move on stone-to-stone, rising.

"There's a spirit in these mountains," Cato says. "What matters is that you climb. Which you've done, now. And then when you think you've done climbed all you can, you climb that last bit and you're there. C'mon now."

For the next few hours, the old guy says nothing as I hear this endless stream of stories and aphorisms ebb and flow in my head. Hymns from childhood, the monk's advice, spoken and unspoken.

We skirt the Wall of Manitou. Overlook. Climb ledge to ledge.

The sky brightens with a yellowish full moon, as we rise up the fast water we now seem to be walking upon.

He grabs my arm strongly and pulls me up a last, ever narrowing, and steeper series of waterfalls and rapids. When we stop for a moment, old man Cato's cataracts appear lit by the moon.

"Over there's the road you came down. You been on it all your life," he says. "Devil's Kitchen's in there, just around the corner from where we're going. Stay out of it. You've come too far to fall again."

Cato turned to face the other direction.

"That man you saw? He calls himself Klokko, just like that other self you imagined yourself to be when you was a kid. Just like your kid, in fact, or at least a growing part of him. Of all of us," he continued. "He, this Klokko-fella, will be coming over the mountain there, meeting up with you on the downward side. It's all sort of the same, I figure. Not like what one expects. It's all about finding a place to rest in the end."

I grab Cato and hold the sleeve of his sweater, as if that could keep him by me. I didn't want to have to finish this alone.

"Up there, in the moonlight?" I ask, motioning as he had. "Is that where we're going?"

I get this feeling that there's a cabin of some sort, red and white and nestled in the blue, moonlit night of the mountain like some idyllic Eden with a woodstove. But I haven't seen it yet. Sort of like deja vu. A möbius strip of time.

I sense a cat in the cabin and almost swoon over a memory of a kitty my Ma once brought home for me and my brothers. We named her BeeBee, for the gun we also wanted. My brothers and I fought over who'd get to sleep with her until Ed decided to give it away because he didn't want the extra expense.

I forgive him for that even though I've always missed that cat.
Beatrice.

Cato's eyes smile but I hear only wind when he opens his mouth.

I reach for his hand again, wanting to thank him for all he's done, for being a good friend. For being a brother.

He's gone.

I keep climbing. I feel safe, as well as cherished and forgiven.
Comfortably dead.

30

Klokko knew he had to move. He'd stolen the guy's clothes, his car. His very identity.

The guy might not know they were the same.

But enough already. Wasn't this to be his own story from here on in?

Klokko scampered across a road in the direction of the higher hills and mountain escarpment he'd come from. If there was anything he knew at this moment, it was that he didn't want to sink lower. It was about time he started home. He had a cat to get to.

He missed the comfort of his failing Mt. Calvary home's red room. The girl he'd pined after. His Olds.

This rocker's life was an encumbrance.

Maybe it was the boots. He wiggled his toes within them. Nice fit, but they came with baggage. Same with the knit trousers and man-panties. Klokko missed the freedom he'd felt running through rain as a naked man in love with Love.

In a snow-ringed glade, lit by the star-studded night sky and rising moon, he stripped off the clothes he'd stolen and placed them by a cairn, then started straight up a steep embankment into the greater darkness ahead.

He felt better.

Klokko knew the moon would come above him to his right. He could be home by dawn. There was a redeeming goodness to the world.

Knackered from the ups and downs of long days, Klokko made his way back into chill water to refresh himself. Then strode up a dirt and gravel road that led past a series of ever-larger mansions, all modernistic with glass fronts and quiet pools overlooking distant vistas from which one could see the reflections of ghostly jet trails, a distant ribbon of water seemingly lit from within. The Hudson.

At one house, dark and ringed in orange police tape, Klokko entered a pool enclosure amidst a dripping, moss-encrusted rock garden. No fence, just bluestone walls carefully laid out and manicured.

Klokko started to again run through all the song titles that had cluttered his head his whole life. Each had a specific memory, from *Little Green Apples* and the belt in his Pa's whipping hand to the girls in kindergarten dancing to *Baby Love*. Ma's soft singing of *Stewball* and *Tom Dooley* as she baked cakes in the kitchen on those nights when Gerard was out late.

He didn't have to get rid of everything. Just deal with them as memories of experiences and not real adventures. Not emotions, really. Mirrored feelings.

Klokko took a stick and moved the blackened leaves and sticks covering the pool and saw something written in mother-of-pearl, maybe mylar. "Twist," in fancified cursive lettering.

He backed out of the pool enclosure and climbed up a steep lawn to the main house, its windows reflecting the light of the moon.

Klokko gave up on trying to sort the jukebox in his head. He was no dream baby, no lion sleeping tonight. Every time he'd try to catch a tune, they'd all cascade into mess. He couldn't even get the steady rhythms going, the *Honky Tonk Women*, *Satisfaction*, or *Smoke on the Water* riffs he'd thought impregnable and as key to his walking, his very breathing, as any underlying skeleton.

He peered in past more police tape at what seemed to be a black stain stretching across otherwise immaculate carpeting. Something bad had happened in there, Klokko knew. He backed away into the surrounding woods. Headed back up the trail towards the escarpment's top.

Why do songs and stories get caught up in our minds with memories of people and places, all such a jumble that we end up mixing tastes and movie scenes and our own past with a wispy tune, a half-remembered lyric?

Klokko saw a strange old boarding-house-like structure up ahead, one light emanating from a downstairs window. He crawled up to it and looked in on a man in purple robes. The guy struck a gong and turned in his direction, pointing a long, elegant finger towards the very direction he was going.

Klokko walked on. He entered a dark forest, carpeted with needles. Drums sounded from his left. When he emerged onto a high meadow, brightly lit by the moon, he saw what looked like hundreds of bodies all dancing and cavorting to undulating rhythms around a raging bonfire.

Klokko stopped and shook his head, then his whole body, like a dog trying to rid himself of fleas. He wondered why he'd stumbled upon the dead man's house. The monastery. Were these things real or simply messages to decipher?

Klokko thought to skirt the drum circle, to find some rutted pathway and get himself up higher. It's hard, he thought, to live with sensitivity AND true righteousness. He wished again that he could have been loved or learned to recognize the love of others, and not just loved others in secret.

He stood up straight, pulled in a deep breath, and walked straight towards the mass of bodies. The closer he approached, the more he heard. Drumbeats in a variety of rhythms. Breath and grunts and the stamping of feat. Awkward laughter. Mortal slapstick.

People parted as he walked among them. No one commented on his nakedness, or even touched him to see if he were cold. Or alive. They simply passed hands around his body as though it were protected by some strange, otherworldly force field, and opened a path to the firepit at their center. He could feel the warmth as he approached.

Could this be what friendship felt like?

"This is for a friend now departed," said a beautiful, frazzle-haired girl by the fire. "You have the right idea, man. We should all lose our clothes like you."

Which they then did, even as Klokko felt himself compelled to keep walking through the crowd and back into the forest, the risen moon pulling him in its path.

He counted as he climbed. Ran the alphabet in his head. Envisioned all the solitaire games he'd played, seeking a clue to his future. This naked climb. This utter, complete strangeness.

It would be a last time. These head games were simply a gesture of nostalgia. He felt warm, deep inside, as he climbed naked up the face of the legendary Wall of Manitou past Overlook.

He reached an overview, a roofless ruin of a giant stone building. It seemed that out before him stretched the entirety of the universe. Twinkling lights punctuated by dark patches where forests, lakes, and rivers lay.

Klokko stood motionless and watched. He knew this place. It *was* Overlook.

"The sad thing about mountains," said a high-pitched voice from the darkness. "Is that you always gotta go down to get up where the heavens touch the land."

Klokko turned and saw the Stand Back on Jim's cap before he saw the man. He felt an overwhelming relief.

"I had a cat once," Jim said, offering his hand. Klokko reached out to take it. "My mom said it made no sense having something domesticated in a wilderness. Said the wild cats would have her as a wife if they didn't eat the sweet thing first."

The old man led Richie onto a stone path leading across a plateau. All tiredness left.

"I stayed by that cat, loved it like I loved my mom. And you know what? It lived just fine," Jim continued. "I've made sure your Beatrice'll be well. She'll be by your side, soon. Noisy critter but sweet, yessir, real sweet."

At a clearing, Jim pointed down a hill towards something shining in the forest.

"Echo Lake, that. Good place for trout," he said. "But that's another trip, my friend. We got to talk, son. Talk while we walk."

As the old man spun stories about his days in these woods, Richie thought about a time he'd long forgot. It was years earlier.

Pa had taken them on a fishing trip to some lake in the Adirondacks. They'd got caught in a rainstorm and rushed into this big cabin guarded by stone lions. The place smelled like balsam. He and Gerard slept on soft cots in a sleeping porch warmed by a big fireplace down in the main room. There were church windows and marbles to play with. Lots of pictures all over the place.

"Was it like heaven, that cabin?" asked the old guy as they edged a series of waterfalls.

"How'd you..." Richie started.

"You don't need to think like the songs anymore, son," Jim said, giving his hand a squeeze. "We're almost there now."

"I'd already figured I could stop," Klokko replied.

The old man smiled.

They reached a pool that smelled of balsam, like that Adirondacks cabin. Richie looked up. There, among a stand of maples, was a suspended light...orange and comforting. He turned to ask Jim what it might be. But the old man had vanished.

Then, in a moment, the man long known as Klokko, now once more growing quietly comfortable as Richie, realized he'd lost half his life in other people's thoughts. He'd defined himself in terms never his own. He'd lost his way.

"God, God, God," he said, tears starting to stream his face. "I'm sorry. I'm so, so sorry I have done this to myself. I'm sorry."

And just then, this Klokko/Richie realized how much his Ma and brother had loved him. And he realized that it was his Pa's love for him that kept him away from the grown man who came to be known as Klokko.

So it goes, he'd once heard. It's all vulnerability. Things would be okay from here on. He just knew it.

And then, he started to climb, one last time, towards the light.

31

I scramble up a steep embankment, all gnarled roots and shale bank. I stand on the road Cato pointed out. I make the last half mile to the cabin I'd seen earlier in no longer than a heartbeat. The moon slips behind a bank of roiling clouds but I know where I am. I'm in dream memory. I know *exactly* where I am.

There's a shortcut through hemlocks to a cliffside lawn in front of the cozy cottage. The sound of rushing water eliminates every last memory I've been hanging onto these past hours since I realized my death.

The place is lit up from inside, casting a warm glow over barren trees, unkempt lawn, and bowing hemlocks. I smell sweet maple wood burning in the woodstove.

There's movement inside.

I tiptoe around the place once, twice, thrice. The cabin is tiny, just a main room and a kitchen plus something upstairs. I see no one. I climb onto the front porch and the thought of sitting in a rocking chair by a blazing fire warms me. I press my bearded face against the windowpane.

I open a heavily painted white door and enter into the cabin's main room, wainscoted floor to ceiling. There's an old couch, covered in an Indonesian print tapestry and a sheepskin. An oriental carpet centers a green-painted, wide-board floor. The glow from the woodstove lights everything; unlit candelabra on two side tables, catty-corner across the room from one another. An old upright piano in the corner.

I glance to the kitchen, similarly wainscoted, with paisley curtains on eyebrow windows. A wood-burning cook stove stands against the wall, the glow of a second fire showing from its round iron top holes upon which a steaming kettle sits, just shy of whistling. There's a kitchen table, covered in a crisp red and white checkered gingham, two straight-backed chairs of a century-old vintage. An old metal and wood hutch painted white. A non-plumbed sink with a hand-filled water container above and slop bucket below. I look in on a hearty stew simmering invitingly in a dark, heavy cast iron stewpot.

Must be one or two rooms like what I've seen upstairs. I knock on the hutch and let out a full-throated "Howdy?!?"

I am dead. I say it out loud: "I am dead. And naked. I am dead and naked and looking for warmth."

I hear a sound. Upstairs.

I move towards the stairs.

On the table are two settings. A bottle of French wine: '67 Châteauneuf du Pape. Two glasses.

Fears attuned, I haul myself up step by worn step.

Nearing the top, waist-level in the stairwell, I note all before me: brown-painted floors, slightly bowed; a single set of drawers, painted dark red; a darkly wainscoted A-frame shaped room mirroring the main room below. There's a peeling, green-painted bookshelf filled with old classics. Then another room just out of view, soft-lit from within the way I recall my childhood room in dreamtime. Must mirror the porch below.

I hear a strange "Gak" noise and go shock-still.

"Yessss?"

A light thump. Padded feet move in my direction. I lean forward.

Before me stands an old cat, skinny and rubbing its back against the doorway, purring.

"Well, whaddya know," I say, climbing up into the room and walking to the aged feline. The room it's emerged from is rustic like the first but dominated by two large full-size beds, a table between them. A glass-shielded candle. Two identical sets of blue striped pajamas and maroon-ribbed bathrobes hang from wooden hooks. Red gingham curtains cover the sole window.

The cat rubs against my naked shin.

It all reminds me of the cabin my Pa grew up in with *his* dad. Early one morning, he and I walked out through fields in the opposite direction from the water. Walked into a deep glade of trees—oaks and elms—where we stopped as a bird lit on a branch beside our heads. He grabbed my hand as several dozen birds settled alongside the one. Then burst out laughing, the birds scattering into the forest over and around us as I laughed, too.

It was then I knew I would have a boy.

I carry the purring cat downstairs through the lamb-redolent kitchen to the main room and its couch. I'm missing everyone. My parents. The band. My women. My son. All those people at my service. Myself.

I feel like everyone's with me here. Could this be the heaven they wanted to imagine me in?

I pour and sip a glass of the wine, fill a bowl of the lamb stew. I've passed beyond regrets.

I seat myself at the piano to play. Just the fingers and keys and whatever arises. None of the old songs. Like it once was, back before success and its burdens.

I make benediction. The only words that come to me are from one of those endless memorials we'd made after the Challenger blew up.

"Sometimes when we reach for the stars, we fall short," I say. "But we pick ourselves up and press on despite the pain."

Music fills the room like a symphony. I am Glenn Gould, Bill Evans. Everything fits into place, including the strange cat sitting on the upright staring down at me, purring.

I moan along with what my fingers play. No words. Not ready. I've stumbled on unwritten hymns, the music of birds and water, what we hear of nature just before we sleep.

A knock comes at the door. The cat rises. Gaks.

32

"You're dead," the naked man in the doorway says, eying Richard Manuel at the piano in pajamas, slippers, and bathrobe.

"I know," Manuel replies. "You must be Klokko."

"Richie."

"Whatever. It's all the same now. There's some pajamas, slippers, and a bathrobe for you, too. Same fit," Richard says, making a tinkling riff on the keys to punctuate his words. "There's lamb stew on the stove. Some awfully fine wine."

"I don't drink," Richie replies.

"I forgot," said Richard. "Just get in here and shut the door behind you. Get yourself dressed and pull up a chair. I'll teach you some four-hand here."

"Beatrice?" Richie adds, shutting the door and leaning down to his purring cat.

The cat-grizzled man and gristly cat greet face to face, noses rubbing.

"Let's not start off awkward," Richard said after a pause. "We got some time together here. Long time. Get settled, my friend."

When the man who had been Klokko returned, Richard motioned towards the couch and made a move towards the rocking chair.

"Nuh-uh," Richie said. "Old rocking chair's got ME..."

He broke into a wide smile which spread, infectiously, to the rock star opposite him.

The two sat and stared at each other, grinning, for a good five minutes before either said more.

"You meet the old guy?" Richie asked.

"I did. Said his name was Cato...."

"Jim," noted Richie. "Had that Stand Back cap?"

"One and the same," added Richard.

"You think it was he who put this all together?"

"It was all ready when I walked in. Whatever...."

Richard moved over to the piano and started to play.

"A lullaby? Cool," Richie whispered. "How's it feel being dead? I mean, I'd always thought I might ask what it was like being a rock star, writing and singing them songs I been singing all these years. But I could care less now."

"Maybe I should ask you the same," replied Richard Manuel. "I always thought I'd be asking *you* all about what it was to be a Klokko. Always scared me, that idea. Carried you around in my head for years, afraid to tell anyone you was in there and... Look, it don't matter to me now, either."

"What you mean?" asked the one who had been Klokko.

"Aren't you dead, too?"

Klokko/Richie pondered a moment.

"I had this idea I had to find love. Had this girl..."

"I met her," Richard said. "Jesse...

"Cute, eh?" Klokko asked.

Richard gave him a school marm's tsking look and Richie/Klokko stood.

"I think I *will* try that wine," he said, heading for the kitchen.

When he returned, Richard smiled and held up his glass. The two clinked.

"Anyway, I found myself naked, running in some rainstorm. Went to sleep and woke up, like, different."

"I know the feeling," Manuel continued the thought, tinkling a few ivories for effect.

"I had this idea I was looking for my Pa, but I guess I was just trying to find what it was that made me click. I don't know. Long journey, strange but, y'know, it feels fine somehow."

"This place," Richard interjected. "I believe it's what they used to call Purgatory. The place we make our atonements from. The waiting room."

"I thought it was Heaven," said Klokko. "I guess I've always mixed the two up."

The cat moved from Klokko to Richard Manuel on the piano bench, purring ever louder now. The pianist looked up, shrugged, then started into a half-classical, half-jazz improvisation on every hymn he'd ever heard.

"I thought I'd find my kid," he said at one point. "Guess you never know what's in store."

Klokko just sat, rocking to the music, looking to the ceiling as his one-time hero, his second self, played on.

"You got the girls from the start. Like Bobby Mason and all the bad asses. You got it all without trying," he finally said over the music.

A moth fluttered along a strip of white paint above his head. His eyes followed it.

"You never felt the pain of *really* loving."

"Where are we, dude," Richard interrupted. "C'mon, stare down that moth. Did the same earlier this day with a whole army of slugs out front of Sid's Ford. This takes time."

"Time. Shit," replied Klokko, finally pulling his eyes off the moth and staring straight into his alter-ego's eyes. "I cried with you when you sang your songs, man. I thought you were IT. I thought you were speaking for me."

"And I was, dude," Richard said, moving forward and reaching a hand over to his mirror's knee. "It's what we do, man."

The two sat looking into each other.

"We both fucked up," Richard Manuel finally added. "Thought we had all the time in the world, all the love to give and take. Didn't notice what there was around us. Or that it all catches up with you."

Klokko grunted, looking down to the floor.

"Fathers, sons, singers, songs. It matters shit," Manuel said, as if suddenly realizing it was useless to be angry when dead.

"I'm a fucking spider," Klokko said, low and almost inaudible. "A spider just like fucking God's an asshole spider."

"A beautiful fucking spider, you mean, weaving perfect webs. Intricate designs."

"Biting," replied Klokko.

"Only when cornered," Richard answered. "You do sound like Hell."

"Always have," said Klokko. "You mind if I sit next to my cat on the bench with you?"

"Sure, dude. And it's *our* cat."

Klokko rose and sat down on the piano bench.

"I saw them slugs, too."

"I know you did. Squished a whole mess of them when you peeled out after seeing me."

The wood fire blazed. The men sipped their wine, identical in pajamas, slippers, bathrobes.

"Why is it those like us always need more love?" Richard said.

He shook his head and played a descending piano measure.

"I know it," Richie replied, putting his hand on Richard's knee this time. "You see what's wrong and stand in front of it, unable to move."

He laughed heartily. Pulled Richard in.

33

When they came to, breath heavy and tears streaming their cheeks, Klokko leaned forward.

"Watch," he said, opening his eyes real wide. "Tell me you love me. Even better, ask me if *I* love *you*."

Richard Manuel did as asked and, sure as shit, Klokko's neck started its turtle thing, first stretching taut and long, then twisting, ever-so-slow and elastic, first one direction and then back, like a corkscrew.

"Dude!" the dead rock star cried out. "Time to learn some four-hand."

"What's the trick to loving?" Richie asked. "Does it exist on its own? Can you really catch and hold the damned thing?"

Richard got up from the bench and moved Beatrice to the couch.

"Don't know," he replied after a moment. "Don't think any of us'll ever know."

Klokko/Richie stretched his fingers and gingerly placed them onto the keyboard.

Up above the lit-up cabin, high over the densely forested Catskill Mountains a short walk away from the Wall of Manitou and the mountain known as Overlook, two owls gyred.

"Cheers," Richard Manuel said. "Let's write some fucking songs about this shit."

Acknowledgments

The first draft of this novel was written during a one-week residency at the Catskill Center for Conservation and Development's Platte Clove Artist's Cabin. Three themes were forged together: my years attempting to chart the Woodstock area's pop history, a series of jovial discussions of an imaginary Catskills character with my talented friends, Steve Gross and Susan Daley, and years of driving the East Coast's back roads. Thanks for the work's patient burnishing must go to the regional weeklies that supported my explorations and writing for three-plus decades, my wife Fawn Potash and son Milo Smart for having my back at all times, and editor/publisher Brent Robison for asking why I never finished what you now hold in your hands.

About the Author

Paul Smart worked as a writer and editor for over a dozen Hudson Valley and Catskill Mountains regional publications in a career that spanned a third of a century. He has published three books, including *Rock & Woodstock* and *With Different Eyes: A Covid Waltz in Words and Images*. He currently lives in Guanajuato, Mexico with his wife Fawn and son Milo, where he is working on a number of film and library projects.

A Request

If you enjoyed this book, its author and publisher would be grateful if you would post a short (or long) review on the website where you bought the book and/or on goodreads.com or other book review sites. Thanks for reading!

Other Books from Recital Publishing

The Berserkers by Vic Peterson
The House of the Seven Heavens by Mark Morganstern
Voices in the Dirt: Stories by Ian Caskey
Our Lady of the Serpents by Petrie Harbouri
Voyages to Nowhere: Two Novellas by Tom Newton
The Lame Angel by Alexis Panselinos
The Joppenbergh Jump by Mark Morganstern
Ponckhockie Union by Brent Robison
Seven Cries of Delight and Other Stories by Tom Newton
Saraceno by Djelloul Marbrook
Dancing with Dasein by Mark Morganstern
The Principle of Ultimate Indivisibility by Brent Robison

And please check out ***The Strange Recital***, a podcast about
fiction that questions the nature of reality.

Printed in Great Britain
by Amazon

28103401R00144